KT-176-274

3 8014 05115 2541

BORN TO TROUBLE

Nelson Nye was born in Chicago, Illinois. He was educated in schools in Ohio and Massachusetts and attended the Cincinnati Art Academy. His early journalism experience was writing publicity releases and book reviews for the *Cincinnati Times-Star* and the *Buffalo Evening News*. In 1935 he began working as a ranch hand in Texas and California and became an expert on breeding quarter horses on his own ranch outside Tucson, Arizona. Much of this love for horses can be found in exceptional novels such as *Wild Horse Shorty* and *Blood of Kings*. He published his first Western short story in *Thrilling Western* and his first Western novel in 1936. He continued from then on to write prolifically, both under his own name and the bylines Drake C. Denver and Clem Colt. During the Second World War, he served with the U.S. Army Field Artillery. In 1949–1952 he worked as horse editor for *Texas Livestock Journal*. He was one of the founding members of the Western Writers of America in 1953 and served twice as its president. His first Golden Spur Award from the Western Writers of America came to him for best Western reviewer and critic in 1954. In 1958–1962 he was frontier fiction reviewer for the *New York Times Book Review*. His second Golden Spur came for his novel *Long Run*. His virtues as an author of Western fiction include a tremendous sense of authenticity, an ability to keep the pace of a story from ever lagging, and a fecund inventiveness for plot twists and situations. Some of his finest novels have had off-trail protagonists such as *The Barber of Tubac*, and both *Not Grass Alone* and *Strawberry Roan* are notable for their outstanding female characters. His books have sold over 50,000,000 copies worldwide and have been translated into the principal European languages. The *Los Angeles Times* once praised him for his "marvelous lingo, salty humor, and real characters." Above all, a Nye Western possesses a vital energy that is both propulsive and persuasive.

BORN TO TROUBLE

Nelson Nye

GUNSMOKE

First published in the UK by Wright and Brown

This hardback edition 2012
by AudioGO Ltd
by arrangement with
Golden West Literary Agency

ISBN 978 1 445 85066 5

British Library Cataloguing in Publication Data available.

Printed and bound in Great Britain by
MPG Books Group Limited

ONE

ANOTHER broiling hot day had practically dragged to its close and I was disgustedly figuring to throw the hull on my pony and head back for town when the rattling stage, northbound from El Paso, pulled up with a screech of brake blocks and stopped just beyond the white picket fence. "Here's the place you was wantin' off at, ma'am," the mustached driver called down from the box.

A woman climbed out. Then Haines cracked his whip and the stage rolled north and was lost in its dust.

I expect I stared like a owl. That was one for the book, him stopping at this place. And for a woman!

I found out I was wrong about that though. With the dust clearing off I could see her better and she wasn't no woman. She was the slickest looking package I had ever clapped eyes on.

Not over sixteen she didn't look in that light, and pretty as a pair of blue boots in some kind of red dress which came snug to her throat. She had a shawl round her head and the hair underneath it in the downslanting sun held the gleam of pure copper.

Hunkered like I was in the shadow of the stable, I don't reckon she could see me with that sun in her eyes. But I could sure see her and she was something to look at. She was standing right there where the stage had left her, peering across the fence toward Cap Murphey's office. And then she spotted Joe Stebbins, the outfit's hostler, where he was slopping white paint on the flag pole.

"Hello there," she hailed. "Is this the headquarters of Company D?"

5

Joe tells her that's right. Never missed a stroke with that brush he was using. "But if it's one of the boys you've come here to see you're jest wastin' your time. They're all out on duty. Duty!" he says, like he hated the sound of it.

Some Ranger's wife, I reckoned, and went back to rubbing soap on my saddle. It wasn't my soap, which was why I was so free with it, figuring I'd got something coming for my time. Five days hand-running I'd been soaking up sun here trying to talk the boss Ranger into signing me on.

"Too young," Murphey'd told me the first day, like twenty wasn't more than half out of the cradle.

"But you took on Tap Gainor," I came back at him.

"When you've had as much experience as Tap's had I'll talk to you. You're a good lad, Jimmie, and a fine hand with horses. I know you can bark squirrels with that hogleg you're packin'. But it just don't add up. I'm sorry."

The next day I told him all the outfits I'd worked for— about the time that big Swede and me tangled at Three Bars, how I'd bossed the wagon at Four Peaks last fall, how I'd busted the rough string for the Hanks boys at Ash Fork. Then I told about the time I had gone with Crump's posse and tracked that Mex horse thief across the malpais and caught him.

Cap listened politely but he wasn't impressed.

"I know all that, Jimmie. You've got plenty of guts. But in our kind of work having guts ain't enough."

"All right," I said. "What else must I have?"

"A Ranger's got to have savvy or he'd damn soon be plant-ed."

"And you figure that's one of the things I ain't got, huh?"

He gave me a slanchways stare and stood frowning. Then his look brightened up. "Let's say you're a Ranger. You're after a hardcase that's just robbed a bank. You've got him tracked to his shack—a place maybe twenty by twelve with four windows. You know he's still got the loot; you know the bank will go broke if you don't fetch it back. You've crept up on the place and now you discover this skunk's not alone;

he's got three-four pals inside the shack with him. It's getting dark fast. What are you going to do?"

"These galoots know I'm around?"

"Only thing you're sure of is—if they do—when it's dark they'll make a break for it and scatter. It's your duty to get the robber but you know the bank will fold if you don't fetch back that loot. Quick now—*what are you going to do?*"

"Reckon I'd call on the bunch to surrender. Tell them to pitch down their guns and come out with their hands up."

"They know you're out there now. They tell you to go to hell. Maybe they slam a few slugs in your direction. It's your move, Jimmie."

"All right," I said. "I injun round to the opposite window—"

"It's too late for that now. In about two minutes it's going to be full dark."

"All right. I kick down the door—"

"And probably get killed," Murphey said, and stamped off.

He wouldn't talk any more about it and for the next two days I might as well have been in Egypt for all the notice he took of my presence. And that was the way we started off this morning.

Then, around ten o'clock, he'd come over to the stables and started pawing through the horse gear hung in the harness room. Way he went over them bridles and cinchas you'd have thought that stuff was his own private property. He never missed a scratch.

He was in a fine ringy mood when he came over to the bench where I sat whittling. "If you're going to hang around you may as well be some use," he mouthed gruffly. "Get what you need from Stebbins and see that those leathers are put in first class shape. When you get that done get some soap and start rubbin'."

I never gave him no back talk. I done it.

After that I went to work on my own stuff. I was soaping the skirts of my saddle when that redheaded armful got off of the stage. I couldn't catch all she said to Joe Stebbins but, pretty soon, there she was going on up the path and rapping on the door of Cap's office. It was open, of course, but she rapped on it anyway. And then she went in.

I finished rubbing my saddle and took the soap to the harness room. I'd have caught up my horse and took off right then except I wanted another look at that redhead. I wondered which of the boys she was married to or, if she wasn't hitched yet, which one of them was sparking her. I hadn't never had many dealings with women but I reckoned to know class when I saw it. And what I had seen made me want to see more.

In about ten minutes Cap Murphey poked his head out and bellered for Stebbins to flag down the southbound stage when it came.

I knew right then I wouldn't have long to wait; and I was right. In just a little while there was a racket like hell emigrating on cartwheels and there it came, swooping out of the Empires with the dust boiling up like a lemon fog.

Stebbins put down his bucket and dashed for the road. I saw the girl come out of Cap's office, pause and turn on the steps for a couple of last words. By this time the southbound's driver had seen Stebbins and had his horses hauled damn near back on their haunches. The girl said, "All right— I'll look for him tomorrow," and came off the steps like a bit of a twister, pantaloons flashing beneath her hoisted-up skirts.

She never looked in my direction but that was all right with me. I got to look at her anyway. She had the reddest hair I ever saw on a chicken. The reddest hair, the whitest teeth and the—

That was when Cap stuck his head out again, just when she was lifting a leg to climb up into that dadburned stage. "*Trammell!*" he yelled.

I like to dropped the damn saddle. Then his eyes picked me up where I was standing in the shadows. "On the double," he grunted.

He was back at his desk when I came into the office. He was fingering some papers that was covered with doodles and

I could tell when he looked up that he was doing some fast thinking. His eyes were bits of shined glass stabbing out of the gloom.

"You still achin' to be a Ranger?"

All I could do was to nod at him dumblike.

"You got any kinfolk around this country?"

"Nossir," I gulped, finally getting my wind back. "Nobody nearer than Flat Rock, Kentucky. My old man had a uncle lived there—or maybe it was a cousin."

"Your father's not living?"

"Redskins got him. Got him and Mom both and pretty near the whole wagon train. That was ten years ago. Soldiers took me back to Fort Apache with them, turned me over to the sutler for raisin'. I stuck it out five years and then I pulled my freight."

"You ever been up in the Cherrycow country?"

"Worked a roundup there two years ago."

"You familiar with Shafts?"

"Never heard of it," I said.

"It's a mining camp. Not far from the ruins of Charleston. Silver, mostly. That girl that was just here came down from there. She wants help. Says she's heir to the Tailholt Mining and Milling Company. Seems to think someone's out to whipsaw her out of it. Father was killed six months ago. Supposed to have been a mining accident—she thinks now he was murdered. Property's being run by the father's brother, man by the name of Shellman Krole, and the mine manager, a fellow named Bender. Lot of funny business going on, mineral concentrates stolen, cave-ins and what not. Girl says they're honest but they can't seem to stop it. Now the uncle's missing. She wants it looked into."

"What's the matter with the local star packer?"

"She thinks he's in with the man that's grabbing the concentrates—"

"And who does she figure is grabbin' them?"

"Local J.P.—some fellow named Frunk. She's guessing, of course, but where there's so much smoke there's bound to be trouble. I've got to send somebody up there."

"You—you mean you'd send *me?*"

Cap frowned. "That girl's got a right to protection. If the local law has broke down up there it's up to us to step in. I don't like the idea of sending a green kid but every one of my boys has got his hands full. If you're bound and determined to be a Ranger—"

I grabbed up his hand and pumped it vigorous. My throat was too full for any words to come. I was remembering the stories of Buckey O'Neill and seeing Jim Trammell, the pride of the Rangers, running the crooks plumb out of Arizona. My heart was pounding my ribs like a single jack.

A grin broke up the harsh lines of Cap's face. Then he let go my hand and said plenty solemn, "I ought to warn you, Jimmie, if this girl's not jumpin' at shadows this is apt to be rough. If I had anyone else—"

"Don't think of it, Captain! You won't never be sorry," I told him earnestly.

"I want you to think a bit, Jimmie. A Ranger never turns back—remember that."

I nodded. "I know the rules, sir. I won't let your boys down."

Murphey eyed me for another long moment. Then he got up with a nod and said, "Raise your right hand."

SHAFTS was on the San Pedro River. I got my first look at it the following evening about an hour short of sundown. Cap had told me, passing on the girl's description, that when I got in its vicinity I could judge how far off I was from it by the sound of fired pistols—and he wasn't far wrong.

Coming in from the north the first place I saw was the little red schoolhouse hunkered off to itself where the end of Burro Alley fans out in a stretch of bear grass. This had all been open-range cow country before the red shirts moved in with their tunnelings and burrowings and, after them, the Long-Tooth Emmas and Faro Charleys that get their knives into every boom.

No one had to tell me that Shafts was booming. I had to duck between buildings three times in five minutes to let shouting riders have enough room to pass. Burro Alley was a red light district with painted faced harridans beckoning and calling from the brothels that lined both flanks of the trail. One canary-haired harlot heaved the bouncers up out of her shift, bold as bull spit, and ran a wet tongue around the rim of her mouth. When I kept right on going she flung such blasphemies after me it's a wonder my ears didn't break into flame.

Passing Jack Schwartz's saloon I came onto the main drag. It was about as noisy a place as I had ever got into. Horses neighing, cattle bawling, galoots of every description and color shouting and swearing in forty different lingos and each one trying to outyell all the rest of them.

Through the thick pall of dust flung up by this traffic I could see the gray shapes of the great rumbling ore wagons grinding their way through the clutter of buckboards. Horse-backers weaved in and out among buggies. One guy with a red dripping Arkansas toothpick made a dive through the crush with three other gents after him. I never did see where he got to but, all of a sudden, some hitched horse gave a screech and went up on his hind legs with five others with him. The tie rail tore loose and came plumb off its uprights and those terrified broncs in the backlash of panic slammed it into a store front whose high wooden awning came down with a crash.

A little of that stuff went a long way with me. There was a bridge to my left and on my right was a hash house. While I was trying to turn my horse in to its rack four whooping cowpunchers in ten-gallon hats tore past on their ponies like hell wouldn't have them, their rocketlike progress punctuated with gunshots. It was every man for himself, let me tell you, with people on foot jumping quick every whichway. I heard more new cusswords in that town in three minutes than a guy could write down in the rest of his lifetime.

I got my gelding wedged in and his reins round the pole but I still had to buck the mob using the walk. It was a regular millrace. Red-shirted Cousin Jacks, cowhands and swampers, mule skinners, desert rats, Mexicans with and without their zarapes, mining men in high laced boots, poker

faced gamblers in tall beaver hats, promoters and pimps—
even a scattering of Indians togged out in the castoffs of
renegade whites. An unending procession, but I finally got
through it.

The restaurant was packed eight deep round the counters.
I had to eat standing but the chuck was good and the java
scalding. The place was run by a Chink in a threadbare
Prince Albert. Crowded against a back window I watched
the San Pedro boiling black and fierce in the stone buttressed
current roaring under the bridge.

The crowds had thinned out some by the time I got finished and I was able to reach my horse in one piece. The
last of the ore wagons had rolled over the rattling planks
of the bridge and were now strung out along the road to the
mill which was off three miles along the river's east bank.
The throb of its banging was like the rumble of thunder.

I looked down the main drag. In the last of the sun its
high false fronts showed a variety of signs: Hogpen Annie's,
The Bellyful Bar, Buskirk's Hardware & Notions, Jack Mc-
Cann's, Gunsmith, Cassie's Casino, Hank's Harness Shop,
Frunk's Mercantile and others too far off to make out rightly
through the still thick haze of the lifted dust.

Untying my horse I climbled into the saddle. A passing
cowhand looked up with a grin. "You must be huntin' for
bear."

"Not sure yet whether it's bear or plain skunk," I said,
kneeing my gelding out into the traffic.

But I knew what he meant. The big Sharps cuddled under
my left stirrup, heavy calibered though it was, by itself
wouldn't have drawn a second look in that country. But
taken together with the sawed-off Greener on the other side,
I expect it looked like a lot of artillery. I had reckoned
that shotgun might invite some attention. I didn't care if
it did.

I was to put up at the Eagle Hotel, Cap had told me, and
I guessed it was time I was hunting the place. It was the
only direct order he had given me. "I never tie a man's hands
with a bunch of red tape. I'm trustin' you," he said, "to get

to the bottom of this thing. How you get the job done is
entirely up to you—consistent, of course, with the traditions
of the Service."

I knew the traditions. I'd been around enough cow camps
to have heard a lot about Rangers. Fact is I'd been raised
up with such after-supper yarning round the campfires. I
knew Burt Mossman, now ranching in New Mexico, had
started them. With thirteen men he'd practically remade
this country at a time when Arizona was the doorstep to hell.
He had fetched the fear of God plumb into the cactus. Had
kicked down more doors and gone in through more smoke
than any other man in the history of the outfit.

I aimed to be another Burt Mossman.

THE first thing, of course, was to find out what I was up
against. The quickest place to learn that seemed to be at the
mine, but I reckoned first of all I'd better find that hotel.

There was plenty such around. I saw the Antler House and
the Miners Rest and, down a little further, was the Cap And
Ball. Then I came to Frunk's Mercantile, a great barn of a
place that looked to carry everything from wheelbarrows to
coffins. I kind of wondered if this Frunk was the one the
girl had mentioned; the guy Cap had said she thought was
getting the concentrates.

I had a hankering to go in and get the measure of what
he looked like, but that was as far as the notion took me.
Folks was lighting their lamps now and the golden glow,
slanching out of doors and windows, played over the boisterous throngs on the walks and lay in yellow bars across the
dust churned up from the potholed road. It was right about
then I saw the sign I was looking for.

It was painted in letters two foot high beneath the second story windows of a pine plank building that had its
behind to the street like it didn't give a hoot whether school
kept or not. And underneath its name it said SHELLMAN
KROLE, PROP. Shellman Krole, I remembered, was the name
of the redhead's uncle, the fellow that was running the Tail-

holt Mining & Milling Company for her—the gent whose disappearance had brought her running to Cap.

It was the very last building at this end of the street. Around its east side, perhaps fifty yards away, the river swung north in a bend that turned the rest of the town up Canada Gulch. Looking that way I could see a livery stable and a bunch of corrals and I judged the stage depot would be somewhere beyond them, though what towns it ran between was more than I could figure. Probably Tombstone and Bisbee—maybe even on south to Douglas. I knew mighty well it never went past the barracks of Company D.

I followed the hotel's east flank around to the entrance and found myself facing a brightly lighted verandah. Ten coal oil lanterns, at two foot intervals, swung shining from hooks along the edge of its roof, their glare intensifying shadows blackly piled beyond the cottonwoods.

There were no horses at the tie rail when I climbed off my own. With all that light in my eyes what I could see of the lobby through the patched and sagging screen looked uncommonly dingy.

I had a feeling right then about this place. I didn't like it.

I was fetching a hand up to hunt for the makings when I looked in again and stopped dead in my tracks.

I couldn't see the whole lobby—couldn't see precious little but the writhing back of a sorrel-topped filly in the grip of some mug who had both arms wrapped around her.

But that was plenty for me. Even before I saw she had both pushing hands wedged against his chest I was taking those warped steps three to the jump.

As I grabbed for the screen I saw her suddenly tear loose of him. But he had her again before I could get the door open, and before I could reach the grinning swivel-eyed polecat someone else had got to him. This guy, a burly red-faced six-footer, made a dive from the stairs that would have shamed any hawk.

The girl ducked clear just before Six Foot struck him. The weight of that leap sent them heels over elbows but Six Foot couldn't hold him. That fancy rigged lady-mauler was wiry as an eel. He was up on his feet before the big guy knew he had got away even. He whirled like a cat and was making for the door when his white-ringed eyes abruptly saw me standing there.

He didn't say "Boo!" He just wheeled clear around and made a leap for the window.

That was where Six Foot got him, about a yard this side of it, with a gorgeous left hook fetched clean up from his bootstraps.

That bird hit the wall like he was going plumb through it. He hung there dazed for a moment with his lamps gone off focus. Then he dropped to the floor like an emptied sack.

I threw a look at the girl. She was white cheeked, still panting, her eyes round as marbles, but it was her, all right— the same nifty armful that had called on Cap Murphey.

TWO

"GOSH, Mister Crafkin! I guess I owe you a debt of thanks but I wish you hadn't done that," she said, like the thought of it really bothered her.

"I ought to've broke his damn neck! Any skunk that would put dirty paws—"

"But you don't understand. He's—"

She let the rest trail off. The big man wasn't paying any attention. He had gone out into another room through an open door beyond the foot of the stairs. While she stood there biting her lips, deep in thought, I heard the clatter of metal, the shriek of a pump that would have probably worked better with a little oil on it. Crafkin came back with a pail of water, his look still riled, and sloshed it over the masher.

It brought him around. He sat up, spluttering.

Crafkin said, "Get up on your feet, you dog, and apologize."

The masher got up. He didn't look to be more than a kid in actual years though his face was rutted with the tracks of vicious thinking. His tobacco-stained mouth was malignantly twisted and the expression of his eyes made the girl pull back sharply.

It didn't bother Crafkin. "Come on," he said, "speak your piece and clear out."

I watched the kid shake his shoulders together and, because I was watching, I caught the bulge of a gun cached under his elbow. He was still pretty groggy and mighty near lost his balance when he bent over for his hat. He jammed it down on his head and cuffed some dust off his clothing.

"Things have come to a hell of a pass around here when a feller can't spark his own girl without—"

"I'm no girl of yours!"

"Ain't you, missy? You was mine right enough until this—"

"Never mind," Crafkin told him. "Speak your piece and get out."

I looked for that kid to snatch for his pistol but he spoke quick enough when the guy started toward him. "I guess I made a mistake. If that's so I'm sorry. I won't make it again."

That was double talk for my money, coming a whole heap nearer matching the look of his eyes than it did to showing any proper repentance.

But it seemed to suit Crafkin. He said, "Now dust. Haul your freight. And don't let me catch you round here again."

The kid adjusted his hat with his eyes glinting baleful. "I ain't forgettin' this, bucko. An' I ain't forgettin' *you*."

He gave his hat a final tug and stalked through the door like an outraged cat.

THE girl thanked Crafkin. "But I wish," she said, "you

hadn't done it. I'm afraid you've piled up trouble for your-self."

"That swallow-forkin' dude?" The big man snorted. "Any time I worry about the likes of him—"

"But you don't understand. He's the one they call 'Short Creek'."

"Him? You mean that rat-faced little sidewinder is the quick-draw artist that rubbed out Buckskin Bert the other night?"

She nodded. "He's filed eight notches—"

"He won't file none for me, don't you worry." Crafkin laughed. "If he comes round here botherin' you again let me know."

The girl turned around then and saw me. "Oh—I'm sorry. I didn't realize . . . If you're looking for a room I'm afraid I can't help you. Have you tried the Antler? Well, there's the Miner's Rest and the Cap and Ball—"

"They're filled up, too," I told her quickly. "If I could stretch out here in the lobby—"

The big man said, "He can shack up with me if you've got an extra cot. I'm pullin' out about ten—got a twenty mile ride to the Diamond U. Cattle buyin' sure ain't the job it used to be."

I saw her give him a look. Saw his lips smile down at her. "I'll be back by tomorrow night more than likely."

"Well . . ." I saw her straighten and square back her shoulders with a deep sighing breath that lifted her breasts against the blue of her blouse. "I suppose I could find an-other cot."

"My name's Jim Trammell," I told her, and took off my hat like I had a few manners.

"I'm Carolina Krole," she nodded. "And this is Joe Craf-kin."

Crafkin shook my fist. "Coming up to try your luck at the diggin's?"

"I might prospect around a little," I shrugged. "Cows is more in my line. Been thinking of buying into a partnership. If I could get me a stake . . ."

Crafkin nodded. "It's a good place to get one."

"I'd better look for your cot," Carolina said, "though what you're going to do about a key I don't know. We don't have any extras."

The big guy seemed to have been sizing me up. "I'll just let him have mine," he said, handing it to me. "Room nine —top the stairs."

He saw the girl's opened. mouth. "I'm not forgettin'," he smiled, "but I can't look at cattle poundin' my ear on a pillow. I've got to be at Diamond U. I've got to go to the Y Bench and look over their gather and I promised Ed Gaines I'd be out to the Pot Hook." He patted her shoulder. "Don't you worry, honey. I'll keep an eye on things."

He grabbed up my hand and pumped it with vigor. "Glad to've met you, Trammell. If you're ever up to Tucson I'll stand you a tall one—I'm goin' to hit the hay now. Move in any time you've a mind to."

"If you're pullin' out at ten," I said, "that's good enough for me. I want to look around anyway."

"Sign the book before you go," the girl said, plainly meaning it for me though she was looking at him. "It's over there on the desk. Put your room number after it."

I took a quick look at Crafkin. He had a good pair of shoulders with plenty of weight behind them, and the style and cut of his garb was what the average cattleman sported. I allowed the guy might be middling handsome if you liked that beefy kind of fried-alive look. I reckoned he wasn't really old—probably not more than forty, but the thing still had me stumped.

I don't know what that guy had but it must have been good. The girl was plenty upset about the thought of him leaving. She couldn't take her eyes off him.

Some guys, I thought, have all the luck.

I picked up her skreaky pen and wrote my name in the book. Thinking she might like to have a few words with him alone, I said I'd go get my roll and leave it there by the desk, that I would put up my horse then and have a look around.

I don't believe that the girl heard a word I said. I couldn't see her face because she had her back to me, having turned plumb around to send a look up at Crafkin where he'd paused on the stairs.

I'd have given a few things to have a chicken like her panting around after me the way she was after that guy. I looked to see a bit of smugness round the corners of his mouth, but all I found was tightness—the same peculiar tightness that was mirrored in his eyes.

Why, I thought, *the fool don't like it!*

I pushed the screen door open. The crickets were in full chorus. Nighthawks swooped about the lanterns. I was half-way down the verandah's steps, still kicking around the queerness of that cattle buyer's expression, when my eyes suddenly jumped to focus.

Some guy was bent over the back of my horse with his arm to the elbow inside of my bedroll.

I was a little bit riled, but not too riled to see straight.

Nobody had to tell me it was that cross-grained bastard, Short Creek. I crept down off those steps like a moccasined injun, ducked under the tie rail and came up right behind him.

"What the hell do you think you're doin'?" I said.

He spun around like a cat and made a pass for his pistol. I slapped it into the bushes and then I plowed into him. But I was a little too hasty and misjudged my aim. His left rang an anvil right back of my ear. A wild swing from his right nearly tore my damn jaw off.

One more of that kind would have folded my tent up but the poor fool got rattled. He dug for the gun strapped beneath his left armpit.

I didn't wait for him to get it. I drove four knuckles up under his chin and his eyes bugged out like they would roll off his cheekbones. He went back on his haunches wabble-legged and stood gagging. I put my fist in his wind and when he jerked forward I brought my left knee right up into his kisser.

I was just getting set to knock him over the tie rail when the snout of a gun dug me hard in the ribs.

I didn't ask any questions. I didn't wait for no orders. I spun like the kid had, smacking hell west and crooked. I caught this new fellow full in the basket.

I watched him go round in a gut-grabbing circle. "Glub glub," he croaked hoarse-like and his knees folded under him. He flopped in the dust like a chicken with its head off.

That was when I first spotted the tin on his shirtfront.

THREE

I WATCHED him roll over and come onto his knees.

He swayed there a moment like he wasn't quite sure if he could get up or not. Then his hands grabbed a hold in the hoof tracked dust. I saw a shudder pass over him.

I could easy have matched it.

Thought of the star this gent had pinned to his shirtfront wasn't the kind of mental exercise most calculated to quiet edgy nerves. This feller would probably be peeved when he got up.

I looked around for Short Creek.

The marshal groaned.

I reckoned the easiest way out would be to show him my own tin. But I couldn't well do that knowing the girl had told Cap this guy was in with the *gambosinos*. It looked like the smartest thing to do would be to make myself scarce and light a shuck for the timber before this sport got in any shape to stop me.

But I couldn't do that, either. Not and maintain the traditions of the Service.

Rangers are expected to be brave. Their reputation is based on never backing off from anything. They are a do-or-die breed that are invariably supposed, no matter what the odds, to pick the nearest crook and charge.

I knew all this. But it was my understanding that Captain John R. Hughes of the Texas contingent frequently used a little guile to strengthen his hand; and the same went for Mossman. I hadn't ever heard anyone question their bravery.

The law of Shafts had quit groaning. He was trying to get up so I went over and helped him. I even brushed off his clothes like I had no hard feelings and handed him his hat. Then I picked up his gun, shook the cartridges out of it, and gave him that, too.

I noticed some other gents had drifted up. They wasn't saying much but they were doing a lot of looking.

So was Jim Trammell.

I reckoned Carolina must have got her signals crossed. This guy didn't look like no kind of a crook. A mite taller than me, he had a muscular swell of neck and shoulder that didn't run to burliness but took away the string-bean look his height might otherwise have given him. Corduroy trousers were stuffed into his range boots. He wore a blue flannel shirt and a gray wipe was knotted tight about his solid neck.

He had corn yellow hair. And a straw colored mustache crouched above a tight mouth that had a solid chin beneath it. He looked every inch a lawman. The way his glance was combing my map wasn't contributing much to the digestion of my supper.

He never glanced at that bunch gathered around us at all. He dropped the gun in his holster and cuffed off his hat. When he'd cuffed it to his liking he re-dented the crown and set it back on his head. He was doing an extra good job of hanging onto his temper.

He had the coldest blue eyes I ever looked into. "If you're ready," he said, "we'll go down to my office."

"All right," I told him, "but I'm taking my bronc along. I'm kind of particular who goes through my belongings."

When we got to his office—a cubbyhole in Canada Gulch

cattycornered across from the stage depot—he dropped into a chair behind his desk, poking out one for me with his foot. "Kind of new around here, ain't you?"

"Just got here tonight."

"Any special reason for picking on Shafts?"

"Just lookin' for a stake."

"Know anyone here?"

"Met a feller named Crafkin a couple of shakes ago but I can't say as I know him. Look," I said, "I'm sorry about taking that swing at you. Expect I was some excited, havin' just caught a walloper goin' through my bedroll. Nothing personal, you understand. When I felt your gun I thought the guy had a crony."

He considered me a while without revising his expression. "What kind of looking gent was he? Ever see him before?"

I said, "He's about my age, take away a year maybe. Duded up like a house afire. Bony face. Lot of fuzz on his cheeks. Lanky."

"You seem to have gotten a pretty good look at him."

"He had a set-to with Crafkin inside the hotel. The girl that runs it told Crafkin this guy was called 'Short Creek'. Seems to be enjoyin' quite a rep in these parts."

"Is there anything in your bedroll likely to invite attention?"

"I think he was just fishing."

"Suppose you fetch your stuff in here."

I got my roll and unraveled it. He looked over my belongings without showing much interest. "Anything missing?"

"I can't think of nothing."

He gave me permission to put the stuff away. When I got my tarp rolled up again I found he was still looking thoughtful. "You haven't any idea what he was after?"

I did kind of have a halfway suspicion that if Short Creek had known about the girl's trip to Cap he might have been hunting something that would hook me up with it. But even to me that seemed pretty unlikely. "Just looking for something he could carry off, I reckon."

"Then why didn't he take your rifle or that sawed-off Greener?"

"Why don't you ask him?" I said.

That made him smile. "There's not more than five hundred people in this camp." The smile went a little twisted. "Ever try to find a needle in a haystack? I've got just one deputy I can put any trust in and I wouldn't trust him much farther than I can throw him. What's this Crafkin look like?"

"Big. Red faced. Black hair and gray eyebrows." I thought back a minute. "Kind of stooped in the shoulders like he'd done a pile of ridin'."

"How old would you put him?"

"I'd say around forty."

He considered me awhile like he was turning that over. I couldn't make out if he knew Crafkin or not. Then abruptly he leaned forward.

"What handle do you go by?"

"My own," I said—"Jim Trammell."

"Any kin to those horse raising Trammells around Sweetwater?"

"Don't know them," I said. "I been punchin' cows for Lou Renzer over in the Four Peaks country." And I had—about a year ago.

"Have you taken up any ground yet?"

"Just got here tonight. Ain't even had time to stable my horse."

He said with his glance coming up from my belt, "You any good with that gun?"

"I reckon I can manage to get a pull on the trigger."

His eyes showed a twinkle. "Would you be interested in a job?"

I done some quick figuring. This fellow, according to what that girl had told Cap, was in with the bunch playing hob with her mine. But women's notions like women's watches is considerably apt to be unreliable. He didn't look like that kind. But on the chance, she might have the right of it, I said, "I'd be interested in almost anything that would be at all likely to get me a stake."

If he was crooked, I thought, that would give him his cue.

But the look of his face didn't change by a particle. I come near snorting my contempt of that girl. I might have known I was a heap better judge of character than any fool chit of a redheaded filly.

It set me back hard when he said, leaning forward, "You wouldn't mind a little risk?"

"Life's full of risk. What kind of job you got in mind?"

I was proud of the way I flung that right back at him. Tough-hombre style like I was ready for anything. Then he jounced me again.

"I could use another deputy. Town's got too big for any three men to handle. There's a lot of riffraff come into this camp and somebody's got to put the fear of God in them before they lug off everything that isn't nailed down."

"But why me?"

"Because I think you've got a head on your shoulders that's good for something besides holding your hat. You've proved to me that you can think in a pinch. You've got plenty of guts and I believe you're honest—and that's what I need, one honest man I can trust."

I shook my head. "I came here to get a stake. I'd be trampin' my whiskers before I made a stake at that job."

He considered me a while like he was chewing it over. "How much money have you got?"

"Not enough to be worth robbin'."

"All right. I'm going to tell you something. You won't make day wages digging round in these hills. All the good ground's grabbed; you'd just be wasting your time. And if by some miracle you happened onto something you'd wind up in some gulch with a hole through your back. I'm not kidding you, Trammell—this camp is plumb rough."

"My feet ain't tender."

"If I thought they were I wouldn't be offering you the job. The point I'm making is that most of what's been found is just float—it's all been gathered. There's maybe twenty or thirty fellows panning day wages out of the creeks. The real money in this camp is coming from the mines—the

Lucky Dog, Bell Clapper, Signal Stope and Tailholt. You can't get into those, not even as a mucker. If you had enough jack you could open up a honkeytonk or a saloon and gambling layout. Slough those into the discard and the only way you can make a stake is to take it at gunpoint or get yourself a job."

I said, "To hear you tell it, nine tenths of this camp is livin' off the other tenth—or trying to."

"That's about the size of it. I think when you've been here a couple of days you'll agree with me. You'll not find many jobs going begging around here. There are too many idle men in this town."

"You won't have no trouble findin' a star packer then."

If my words put him out his face didn't show it. He even managed a smile. "No, I won't have any difficulty locating help. I can put my head out the door and get a crowd in three minutes. Riffraff," he said. "The lousy camp is full of it."

He got up and shook my hand and actually looked a little sad. "If you change your mind look me up again, will you? The job pays two hundred and fifty a month. Including a casket if you make the wrong jump."

I RETIED my bedroll to the back of my saddle. I took off my hat and ran a hand through my hair and saw by the stars the night was crowding ten o'clock. There was still a bunch of people on the street, a lot of traffic. But I couldn't have told you what or who. I was still back there in that office with the marshal, hearing him say two fifty a month.

I wasn't surprised. I was downright astounded. I knew damn well I couldn't make two fifty in any other way except by sticking someone up. And, what's more, I knew *he* knew it.

And that crack about the casket.

There was a heap more to this than met the naked eye and, as a Ranger, I reckoned I ought to give it a looking into. Two fifty for a deputy! I'd have bet my pants Cap Murphey himself wasn't making half that!

Was that doggone redhead right after all? Had I read this guy wrong?

I didn't know what to think, hardly.

Maybe, I thought, if I would circulate around I might pick up a line on this business. One thing was sure. I didn't like even a little bit the way he'd dragged 'casket' into his talk. It sounded too much like a threat, for my money.

But that didn't make much sense to me, either. If he'd meant it as a threat then the guy was a crook, and he sure didn't look like no crook to me. He had the bold lively features of an honest square-shooter—and look at the way he'd brushed over my slugging him. Would any crook have done that?

Another thing. Even if this guy was the worst kind of crook, what reason would he have for threatening me unless he'd found out I'd come up from Cap Murphey? I didn't see how he could have found that out no way; and I hadn't even been a Ranger till yesterday. No marshal would be fool enough to threaten a guy just because he didn't want to take a job as his deputy!

I reckoned I was getting a little over-excited, dreaming up threats where no threats existed. Suppose he *had* found out I was a Ranger, or suspected it—would a crook have tried to hire a guy he thought was a Ranger?

I untied the reins and climbed aboard my horse. He moved out into the street without urging, tossing his head like he was getting plumb tired of waiting around for his supper. I let him pick his own way, just to see what he would do, and he lost no time packing me over to the livery where his exasperated nicker finally fetched out the hostler.

I said, "Give him a little roll, then rub him down. Feed and stall him."

The hostler nodded and I set off uptown.

I wasn't what was known as a drinking man but it seemed to me the best place to go if you were hunting information was a barroom. Of course, I could go to the girl and tell her flat out I'd come up from Cap to look into her troubles. But that didn't strike me as being extra smart.

In the first place, I thought, she probably didn't know much about what was going on anyway. Whatever she might tell me stood a mighty good chance to get me mixed up worse than ever. I already knew, from what she'd said to Cap, that she suspected this guy Frunk and the marshal of being mixed up in it. And maybe they were. But what about her uncle? True, she'd said he'd disappeared, but that might mean anything or nothing. And what about this Bender who was supposed to be running the property for her? She'd already told Cap she was sure they were honest. But that didn't make them so in my book. Seemed like I'd get further quicker if I started from scratch.

And, besides, she was a woman. A damn good looking one, I was ready to admit, but prey just the same to all the fool notions that fill women's heads. And she'd probably talk and let something slip. It was my experience that women usually did. I'd have my work cut out for me if it ever got around this camp I was a Ranger.

I would be a heap smarter, I thought, to keep away from her. And the further away the better. There was no place for a woman in a Ranger's life and I sure didn't want to make no fool of myself.

I went into Jack McCann's, a gambling house and saloon that was just across the road from the Eagle Hotel.

The place was well filled, mostly with cattlemen and cowhands in from the range for a shot at the tiger, but there was a sprinkling of red shirts scattered through the crowd and, like as not, a few rustlers.

The games were going full tilt with a circle of watchers impatiently waiting their turns at each rig. But the bar was the place where the jaws were wagging and a good listener, I thought, should be able to hear plenty.

I was right about that, but it was mostly talk about conditions and cattle and the arguments were all over women and horses. It didn't take me more than a quick ten minutes to savvy I'd got into the wrong caboose.

I clanked my spurs outside and up the warped plank walk until I found myself before the Bellyful Bar—Brian Gharst,

Prop. This, I saw right away, was more like it. The smells
and clatter-bang noise of the place came against me like the
flat of a hand, even before I shoved through the batwings.
This was a mining man's hangout and the brogue was so
thick you could slice it.

A guitar picker flanked by a couple of fiddlers playing
Chicken in the Straw was perched on kegs at the back of the
place and a mob of sweating hardrock men were loping their
squealing partners round and around a twelve-foot square.
Gamblers were doing an efficient business of parting mis-
guided fools from their bankrolls and tobacco smoke swirled
round the lamps in blue clouds.

A fat little chick in a one-piece dress that didn't much
more than cover her navel got hold of my arm and tried
to tow me upstairs. But I had my aim firmly pinned on the
bar and after a couple more tries she went after someone
else. And that was when I got my first sight of Soledad.

She was up on the balcony, just behind the place where
the low spindle rail was hid behind the colors of a Mexican
zarape. She was Mexican, too—or maybe half Spanish, blue
black hair piled high with a comb. She was supple and tall
with the shape of a willow, lips red as cherries and a red
dress to match them.

She stood like the daughter of some rich hidalgo, black
glance playing scornfully over the crowd.

She was a looker, all right. No mistake about that.

Her eyes caught me watching her. Someone bumped into
me. I said "Sorry," without looking away from her. I saw
a smile quirk her lips, saw them murmur something. And
then a guy in a plug hat stepped up to the rail and raised
both hands and the talk fell away.

"Gentlemen," Plug Hat said, "I give you Soledad!"

Hands clasped, feet stomped. The building shook with the
roar of raised voices. The girl moved to the rail and there
was a thunderous quiet. A guitar flung the opening bars of
Jalisco across it, and she sang.

Her husky voice was enormously stirring. When she quit

the crowd went wild with applause. "More!" they cried.
"More! More!"

She put both hands to her lips, and was gone.

It was effective as hell.

My pulses still throbbed with the sound of her voice when
someone touched my shoulder. "Lady wants to talk with
you."

Tinhorn was written all over him. He had the typical
small-time gambler's look—clothes, mannerisms and everything else.

"What lady?" I said.

"The one that just sang. Soledad."

"And what would she be wanting to talk with me for?"

"How should I know?" It was plain he thought I was a
fool to stand arguing.

"Where is she?"

He jerked his head and set off toward the bar's far end
where, under the balcony's overhang, a heavy door was set
into the room's back wall.

"I didn't get it. I couldn't see what she would want with
me—I wasn't that vain of my looks by a long shot. But I
followed him. Stood with churning thoughts while he opened
the door.

There was no room beyond it. Nothing but an alley choked
black with shadows and the penetrating chill of the river-
damped night.

I looked at the guy, the knowing smirk on his face. He
stood aside, his eyes shining. "Knock twice on the door at the
top of the stairs."

I stepped out, never thinking what a target I made. If I
hadn't been turning to ask where the stairs were I'd have
caught it dead center.

I heard the *chunk!* as its blade struck the slammed-shut
door.

FOUR

Sweat poured out of me.

My eyes dug into the roundabout shadows and the gun in my fist was ready to cough at the first sign of movement. Only there wasn't any sign. No racket aroused by panicky haste, no stealthy tread of a cautious withdrawal. Not even the rasp of a stifled breath. The loudest thing in that trash strewn alley was the muffled thud of my pounding heart.

By the time it got quiet I had hold of myself, had quit building wild notions and was able to reason. Whoever had tried to stop my clock had not stayed around to find out if he'd done it. That much I was sure of. The passage was empty.

But I'd been foolish enough for one night. I came out of my crouch with a straining care. I kept my gun gripped ready in case I was wrong and, bending again, felt around with my left till I got hold of a rock. I listened one further moment, then tossed the rock out into the murk just beyond where the rickety stairs climbed skyward perhaps twenty paces away to my left.

It struck with a tincanny clatter.

I counted to a hundred and twenty by ones and, satisfied then I had the place to myself, turned around and took hold of the thing in the door.

It was a bone handled knife with a razor-sharp blade. Its point was driven so deep in the wood I had to holster my pistol and use both hands to budge it. Even then it took all my strength to get it loose.

I could see a lot better now my eyes had got used to the dark, but I had to know something my eyes couldn't tell me. I thrust the knife in my belt and took hold of the door-knob. Very quietly I turned it and cautiously pushed.

The door was locked.

So he was in on it, too. Or wasn't he?

I could probably find out by going up those stairs.

Good judgment told me to let well enough alone and get out of that alley while I still had a chance. Somebody in this camp didn't want me around and had done their best to get me planted. *Why?*

There were only two answers to that one. Settling a grudge or they knew what I was here for. I wasn't too sold on the grudge theory. Nor I didn't see how anyone could know what I was here for unless they also knew the girl had gone to Cap Murphey. I didn't see how they could know that, either.

I went up the stairs and pushed open the door. I dived in quick and slammed it shut behind me.

It surprised me a little to see the place was rigged out as an office. "You've changed some," I said, "since I heard you sing."

He wasn't embarrassed. He even showed me a grin. "Put that popgun away and cool off."

"This gun stays right where it's at," I said, "till I find out what kind of game you're dealin'. It better be good. You don't look like no red-skirted warbler to me!"

"That was just the come-on—"

"Was that locked door a come-on? And that guy in the alley?"

But he waved it away. "I've got a job for you. I didn't want the whole town knowing my business—that's why I had Spence dish up that guff about a lady. I'm Brian Gharst—"

"I don't care," I said, "if you're Theodore Roosevelt! You take a damn funny way to make a man's acquaintance and if I get any more of these tossed in my direction some-one's like to wind up in a pine plank box!"

I slammed the point of the knife deep into his desk and

the haft of it vibrated like a prodded rattler. It might have been a rattler by the way he stared down at it.

"Where the hell did you get that?"

"Out of that door by the foot of your stairs. And if it had come any closer I'd of been a cooked goose."

He pulled his stare off the knife and rummaged my face. He was not a big man as gents go in this country, but there wasn't nothing puny about him. He had short bowed legs and was so thick through the shoulders it gave him a queer top-lofty look like a farm wagon swaying under a double load of hay. He wore steel-rimmed cheaters over bleached-out blue eyes and his brush of black hair was getting thin on the top and pretty gray around the edges. But he was not an old man and there wasn't any rust got on the wheels in his think-box.

"You trying to tell me someone threw that thing at you?"

I said, very patient, "It wasn't thrown at no chipmunk."

He looked at me, baffled. "But why should I—"

"Look," I said. "What would *you* think if some pasteboard fanner stepped up to *you* in some dive you hadn't ever been in before with a line some warbler was wantin' a talk with you and then, quick as ever, he got you out into an alley where light from the door showed you up like a barn afire—"

"Good Lord!" Gharst said. "Is that what happened?"

"I'm tellin' you, ain't I? All I'm askin' you now is what you figured to gain by knockin' off a broke drifter—"

He said with a convincing show of earnestness, "Believe me, Trammell, I had nothing to do with this—"

"You're wantin' me to believe the bird that threw this knife had no connection with you?"

"I can't help what you believe, but it's the truth," Gharst said. "I wanted a talk with you that would be private and not be known about. I didn't figure my name would have any drawing power, so I told Pete Spence to say that Soledad—"

"What did he slam that door for then? Why'd he have to lock it?"

"I don't think he knew there was anyone in the alley—

I certainly didn't. You have to slam that door to get it properly shut. We always keep it locked."

"It wasn't locked when he opened it."

Thought wrinkled up his cheeks. "It should have been." He sat down behind his desk, stretched out his legs and looked at me. "I don't know what to say to you. I know this business looks suspicious as hell. Nothing I can tell you is going to make it look better. There's a lot of riffraff in this camp. One of them, prowling through that alley just as you stepped out, may have flung that knife for whatever he could get from your pockets."

I gave him a grin.

"Hell's fire!" he said. "What else can I think?"

"Don't ask me to put words into your mouth. I find it damned hard to swallow that some guy happened by just as your understrapper sent me into that alley!"

"You find it easier to believe the guy was out there waiting for that door to open? That he was tied in with Spence? That Spence and me and this bird had it figured to plant you? When I'd only just seen you and Spence didn't know—"

"Where?"

"Where what?"

"Where had you seen me?"

"Where you stood looking up at her. Down there in the barroom. I was out on the balcony when the girl was singing. We both were. It was Spence introduced her—remember?"

That was true. Spence had. But I still didn't like it. I kept remembering the way Spence had slammed that door. The way he had locked it.

"All right," I said, letting him think he had sold me. "So I'm here. What's the rub?"

He got a cigar from his pocket and bit off the end, his eyes checking over me while he got it to going. He said through the smoke, "I'm looking for a fellow I can put some dependence in. I expect you can use a little ready cash, can't you?"

"If it don't involve putting my neck in a sling."

"No danger of that. You haven't a job now, have you?'

"I only pulled in about three hours ago."

"Good," Gharst said, rolling the cigar across his mouth. "You're just what I need for this business. I don't guess you'll mind a little risk if you're well paid for it?"

"Let's get down to brass tacks," I told him. "How much and for what?"

There was something strange in his look right then and something nervously careful in the way he got up and went over to the door I'd come in by and stood a long moment with his ear up against it. He even toed up a rug against the crack underneath it, and then he catfooted over to the door giving onto the balcony and listened there awhile, suddenly jerking it open and poking his head out before he came back and flopped into his chair.

"I guess you think I've got a screw loose, but you don't know this town like I do—even the goddam walls've got ears. This job calls for a man who ain't known around here; above all for a man who can't by any stretch of the imagination be tied up with me. That's why I have to be careful—"

"What about Spence?"

"Spence will keep his mouth shut. I'll see to that. Maybe I'm being unduly cautious—I was a lawyer back East." He put another light to his thin black cigar, puffed it awhile, and then he bent forward. "The big cheese in this camp is a fellow named Frunk. He owns about half of this town right now, including Frunk's Mercantile, the Cap and Ball, the Antler House, three or four of the drink and chip emporiums and the Signal Stope Mine. But that ain't enough for him—he wants the whole works and, as things stand now, he's well on the way toward getting them."

"That don't suit your book?"

"I'm going to bust that woodchuck if it's the last thing I do."

"If he's that big a frog you'll have your work cut out to skin him. Does he own this place?"

The light flashed back from his steel-rimmed glasses. "No

—nor he ain't about to. Not if he hires every crook in the country, including that stinker we've got for a marshal. I will burn the place down before I let him get it. Not that he hasn't been trying. He keeps the stage robbed so regular a man can't send a thing out of this camp. Which is how he makes sure we'll have enough cash on hand to make the weekly stick-up worth his crowd's time."

"Plays rough, eh?"

"Hardly a week goes by that my place ain't stuck up. But I can play rough myself, as he is going to find out."

"And that's where I come in?"

Gharst nodded. "You'll be the start. I want you to get a job with him. I want you to work your way into his confidence till you get enough dope to pin the deadwood on him. I'll take it from there."

"And that's all you want me to do?"

"That's all you need to worry about now. You come through with enough stuff to fix his clock and I'll see that you're well taken care of."

"I'll see to that part myself," I said. "I'll expect a guarantee of good faith every Saturday. I ain't stickin' my neck out for promises."

He knocked the ash off his smoke and nodded. "Two hundred every Saturday—you can get it from Soledad. You're going to have to keep clear away from me or Frunk will get wise. He's no fool, believe me. Two hundred a week and a thousand above that when you bring me enough stuff to pin back his ears."

"Any particular kind of evidence you're wantin'?"

"Get anything and everything you can on the bastard. I want his clock stopped. I want enough stuff to do it."

"To convince you, you mean? Or somebody else?"

"You don't have to convince me. What I want is enough to fetch the Rangers in here—and don't write me down as a sucker. I want the deadwood on Frunk inside of a month. If you can't do it in that time I'll get someone else."

He fetched out his wallet and peeled off fifty bucks.

"Here's a little cash to get started. Don't come to me till
you've got what I want."

"Suppose I have to have help?"

"If you have to have help you're no good to me."

He turned out the lamp and I went down the back stairs.

FIVE

BUT not without some disquieting thoughts.

These had nothing to do with the depths of the night, with
the creaking of stairs or with the blackness of shadows
wedded one to another in the gloom of that alley. The cold
glitter of stars, the damp smell of the river were things I
noticed no more than I did the rowdy sounds of carousal.

I was being dealt cards from a stacked deck, and knew it.

Everything Gharst had told me about Frunk could be true.
He could honestly have been hiring me to do a job for him.
But this could well be a trick to throw me off my guard, to
shut my mind against the shape of things to come, the easier
to steer me up against some blank wall.

I wasn't trusting that fellow no farther than I could heave
him.

Trammell he'd called me. And where had he learned that?
I hadn't told him my name was Trammell. I'd told the
marshal, right enough, and I had told Carolina. But not
Brian Gharst.

There was a polecat smell in the vicinity of this deal that
was beginning to get my hackles up. It was commencing to
get inside of my noggin that this fellow Gharst might be a

pretty sly article; and for a couple of cents, I told myself, I would go ram that fifty bucks up his adenoids.

Then my mind got to working. There was a number of things about Mr. Gharst that a first class Ranger would want to have answers to, and maybe that job would be the smart way to get them. Since he knew my name there was a whopping good chance he might also know what I was here for. Maybe he didn't but, whether he did or not, I'd be a lot more likely to get my teeth into something I could use if he figured I was stringing along with him.

That was the way it looked to me when I came out of the alley onto the main drag's north walk. The Chinaman's was directly in front of me across the street and the traffic had toned down to where there wasn't but three horsebackers in sight, ranch hands, I reckoned, on their way out of town.

I quartered across the hoof tracked dust and stepped onto the south walk in front of Frunk's Mercantile. It was getting about time I hit the hay, but I thought before I did so I might just as well catch a look at Mr. Frunk. It seemed queer to find a general store keeping open this late, but everything else was open; there wasn't one dark front on the whole main drag.

I went up three steps and into the place. The town's boardwalks were practically empty now but ten or twelve fellows in various garb were still holding forth inside the store, only one of them actually there on business. The rest were sitting on kegs and boxes whittling and smoking and chewing the fat. Three or four of these birds looked like pretty hard customers, more especially the one in the bullhide chaps. He was a stoop shouldered specimen with rust colored hair and a hard bitten face bad in need of a shave.

I took a perch on a crate of mining machinery and couldn't make out if this was Frunk or not. With an idle ear cocked for the gab of the rest of them I watched him limp back of the counter and reach himself down a can of high priced sardines. The clerk never batted an eye as this party scooped a fistful of crackers from a box and, going back to the counter, cleared himself a seat amid a clutter of yard goods by knocking three bolts of printed cotton on the floor.

He got a knife from his boot-top and, cutting open the can, slipped a brace of dead fish between a couple of crackers and set there swinging his legs while he munched them.

This guy was no puncher. He might be got up like one but he had all the earmarks of a privileged character. He absorbed all the talk but didn't bother to take part in it, not even when the relative merits of two chippies took over the conversational floor. He just chewed his sardines and swung his booted feet, alternating this performance with audible gurgles from a bottle he'd had the clerk fetch him.

Then one of the gabbers twisted his head around to ask, "What's Bucks Younger figurin' to do about Short Creek?"

"Why'n't you ask him?" Rust Hair said, and a fat man next to the asker snickered.

"You mean he ain't takin' you into his confidence?"

"Just on the big things, Roy," Rust Hair said. "How deep have you got that hole down now?"

"Eighty-five more or less."

"Hit anything yet?"

"Not enough to chink the ribs of a sand flea—"

"That why you got four guys with shotguns settin' on it?"

"Well . . ." The fat man looked sheepish at the laugh the rest gave him. "That's just common sense. I've sunk a pile of good dollars into diggin' that hole. You know how rough things is gettin' round here. What with all these claim-jumpers prowlin' the hills—"

"You're right," a voice said; and Roy broke off, twisting his head. The others twisted theirs, too. Turning my own I caught a look at the fellow.

Coming in from the back room, this jasper was so tall he had to bend his head to keep from smacking his nose on the lintel. With his florid face and yellow goatee, togged out the right way he might have passed for George Custer. On a horse and flourishing a sword he could have made it. He had the same bright yellow hair. The same pair of eagles was looking out of his eyes. Only it was hard to think of Custer in a flat-crowned hat. It was even harder to picture him in string tie and Prince Albert. And this guy's size wasn't right.

He was big all over. He had a big voice to match it.

"You're absolutely right!" he boomed, nodding his head vigorously. "It's getting so around here that a man of any substance takes his life in his hands every time he draws a breath. I don't know what's come over this place, or where all these crooked drifters are coming from, but it's time, I say, this camp was cleaned up. You knew Andy Tedron was killed the other night? This morning they found poor old Joe Gantry with his head stove in—killed in his own bed! Murdered, by godfreys! I tell you, if I didn't have so much invested around here I would take the next stage and get clean out of the country."

He gave me a look, swiveled his eyes back to Roy. Seemed like to me Roy was looking a little pale, but maybe it was just the light that made his eyes look so funny. He opened his mouth like a fish but he didn't say anything.

The sardine eater, chewing, grinned from the counter.

Frock Coat said, "The Lord knows I've got all the stuff I can take care of now but as a token of my friendship, Roy, if you're wanting to get out I'll take that claim off your hands. Would three hundred dollars pay for what you've put into it?"

The fat man squirmed.

"The Lord giveth and He taketh away," intoned Frock Coat, in the manner of a man doing his thinking out loud. "A wise man will hear, and will increase learning. But fools despise wisdom and instruction."

Rust Hair said, still chewing with gusto, "Let us wait for blood. Let us lurk privily for the innocent. Let us swallow them alive as the grave; and whole, as those that go down into the pit."

With his piercing gaze on the fat man's face, Frock Coat nodded. " 'For their feet run to evil and make haste to shed blood. And they lay in wait for their *own* blood; they lurk privily for their *own* lives'."

And he nodded again. "Lot of comfort in the Book. You ever felt the power of the Word, Roy?"

The fat man's cheeks were a fish-belly white. I could see sweat gleaming in the creases of his jowls.

"Wisdom crieth without!" thundered Frock Coat. "She uttereth her voice in the streets. She crieth in the chief place of concourse, in the openings of the gates."

From his perch on the counter the sardine eater chuckled. " 'But ye have set at nought all my counsel. I will laugh at your calamity. I will mock when your fear cometh.' "

The fat man's tongue crept across dry lips. His glance searched the roundabout faces despairingly.

Frock Coat turned and his lambent eyes, after brushing across mine, abruptly stopped and came back and looked at me inscrutably.

"Good evening, Brother. I don't recall your features. Are you new to this camp?"

"I ain't been here long."

"Are you looking for lodgings?"

"I got a room at the Eagle."

"Cow puncher, aren't you?"

"Expect I could tell which end takes the grass in."

He considered me a moment, thoughtfully fingering his goatee.

"Mister Frunk—" Roy gulped hoarsely, "could you give me as much as fifteen hundred?"

Frock Coat's stare hung onto mine a mite longer. Then he said to the fat man over his shoulder, "That's a lot of money, Roy, for just a hole in the ground."

"But it's in the right section—Hell, it's smack up against your Signal Stope! The vein is—" The fat man peered at him and swallowed. "W-would you give me a thousand?"

Frunk shook his head. "I'm a one price man, Roy. I made the offer as a friendly gesture, not because I've any use for your claim. If you know anyone who'll give you more, you'd better take it."

Rust Hair wiped off his mouth and said, "You hear what happened to that guy the other side of you? That feller

Jimson? Fell down into his shaft and broke his neck. Just happened—less than two hours ago."

Frunk smiled at the fat man. "I thought probably you'd heard about it, you looked so daunsy. I remember saying to myself, quick as ever I saw you, 'There's a lad that could do you some real help, Gideon. This business of Jimson hath ground his hopes beneath the nether millstone.' I could read your thoughts. I could even understand them, because a thing like that could happen to anyone. So I made you the offer. I figured you wanted to get away from this place."

There wasn't much doubt but what Roy wanted to now. He was a plenty frightened man.

SIX

The silence stretched like a violin string while his bulging stare went from face to face with the last gleam of hope finally flickering out of it. Fear and shock and desperation levered him onto shaky legs. Some fatal clarity of insight must have spread that blanched look across his cheeks.

With chin on chest he fumbled the makings but his clumsy hands couldn't build the smoke. The paper wouldn't roll in his fingers. It twisted and tore and fluttered out of his grasp.

A kind of convulsion writhed through his shoulders and his lifted head showed the face of a corpse. The blind eyes stared unseeingly at Frunk. The stiff lips said without inflection, "That's right. That's right. I'm gettin' out."

I got up off the packing crate. "Don't be in no hurry, Roy. You better go home first and think this over."

The fat man probably never heard me.

But the rest of them did. It got so still in that place I could hear the distant clink of glasses, a woman's high laugh coming out of McCann's.

It was like being faced by a ring of watching vultures. I saw the heads twist around on their scrawny necks. I felt the curse of their stares digging into me. I saw three dropped hands spread above holstered pistols.

Frunk's mouth softly chuckled.

"Go on, Roy," I said. "You go home and think it over. If you feel tomorrow like you want to sell out—"

"No."

"No what?"

He never moved his head. "I'm sellin' out now." He kept watching Frunk with eyes that didn't see him. I don't guess they saw any part of the room. I don't guess they could see across the rubble in his mind.

I had to wake the guy up. I took hold of his arm but he shook me off. "I know what I'm doin'."

He didn't sound like it.

But Frunk with a grin moved away behind the counter and got out a printed form, a grubby pen and an ink well. "Here you are, Roy."

Roy moved up to the counter like a guy in his sleep.

"You damn fool!" I said. "You going to let them bluff you?"

He dipped Frunk's pen in the ink and scratched his name on the paper. Then he dropped the pen like it burnt his fingers. But he couldn't get his eyes any higher than Frunk's belt. Sweat made an ashen shine on his cheeks. He licked his lips several times and finally muttered, hardly audible, "If you'll give me my money—"

"Money?" Frunk said. "You forgotten that bill you run up here last winter?"

The fat man gaped like a poleaxed steer. "But—but—it wasn't for no three hundred dollars!"

Frunk got out his ledger, flipped a couple of pages. "That's right. Here it is right here. Two hundred and forty-nine dollars and fifty-three cents exactly."

Roy staggered back.

"You want an itemized statement?"

"No . . . No," Roy muttered. "Let me have the fifty dollars."

"Come around in the morning. If I—"

"But I want to get onto that southbound stage!"

It was a desolate whine the way Roy said it. Frunk said contemptuously, "The southbound don't pull out till 4:00 a.m. If I give it to you now you'll have it guzzled away by then and be a charge on the town—"

"I won't—I swear I won't—May God strike me dead if I touch a stinkin' drop!"

"Very well," Frunk said. "You all heard him, gentlemen." He counted fifty silver dollars into a poke and passed it over. Like a hungry cur with a bone, the fat man caught it up and with it hugged to his chest went staggering from the store.

Frunk's eyes looked into mine. "I can see you don't approve of us, Brother. Because you're new to this camp I'm going to venture a little advice. You'll see a lot of things more ugly but if you're smart, my friend, you'll whittle your own stick and let the rest of us whittle ours."

There were a lot of things trembling on the edge of my tongue but I managed to keep them hobbled. It was probably just as well, the way that sardine chewer was eyeing me. What Frunk had said was plumb right. I wasn't the fat man's keeper. I was in this camp for one purpose only, to get to the bottom of what was going on at Tailholt. It was time I was remembering that and playing my cards according.

I put away my scowl and tried to show more friendly. I said, "That's damn good advice and mighty fittin' for a gent that's drifted off his home range. You look like a pretty big mogul to me. How's this town fixed for jobs? Know anythin' I could handle?"

"What sort of a job are you looking for, Brother?"

"Any kind that pays well. I don't aim to work for peanuts." I took a slap at my gun. "I'm pretty handy with this thing. Any chores along that line you want taken care of?"

Frunk sucked in his breath and looked at me distasteful like.

"I'm afraid not, Brother. We'd like to make this camp a quiet and peaceful place to live. We wouldn't care to do anything that might encourage more rowdyism."

"Well," I said, "I reckon—"

"If you're handy with that gun," Frunk said, "you'd better get in touch with our marshal."

"How much you payin' this star packer?"

"The marshal of Shafts is paid by our Better Business Bureau—"

"How much?"

"I understand he is paid five hundred a month and allowed a little over for expenses."

I whistled. "Five hundred smackers for—"

"We consider the money well spent," Frunk said smoothly, "where it tends to put a curb on the camp's undesirables."

"This guy gets the job done?"

"There's always room for improvement," he said thoughtfully. "But taking the view of Better Business, the most of us believe he's doing all we can expect of him, shorthanded as he is and with at least half this camp out to do the other half."

"The haves and the have-nots, eh?" I said.

"I suppose that would tend to be the popular inference. As a matter of fact, there are quite a few Haves in the local setup whom I would not regard as being at all 'solid citizens.' Every town has its balance of power, a kind of status quo maintained to insure that current events run along more or less in their established pattern."

"And this marshal's chief concern, I reckon, is to see that it continues to operate."

Frunk smiled. "I guess you'll have to ask him about that. You'll find his office in Canada Gulch, just across the street from the stage depot."

"And what if he don't want to hire me?"

"In that case, Brother, I'd suggest you leave town."

ACCORDING to the sky when I stepped out of Frunk's store I had been in this camp just about five hours and, while I hadn't got much forwarder with the thing Cap Murphey had sent me here to do, I'd gathered plenty of food for reflection.

The marshal had offered me a job as his deputy—as one of them, anyway, at two fifty a month; half what he was getting, according to Gideon Frunk. Then Gharst had gone to considerable bother to offer me a job spying on Frunk at two hundred a week, with a thousand extra thrown in if I could wangle it so he'd get caught by the law. Frunk, himself, hadn't offered me anything but words.

He was a slick talking article and, from what I had seen of him, I was pretty near ready to accept Gharst's estimate —not that I rated Gharst any higher. They were both crooks for my money, and half the cussedness bothering this camp might well be the result of a struggle for power with Gharst on the one side and Frunk on the other.

A first class feud could throw this camp in a shambles. But my job was Tailholt and, up to right now, I hadn't learned one thing I hadn't known before I started. According to the girl, her father had been killed about six months ago. In a mining accident—apparently. Then she'd started losing concentrates. She'd implied Frunk was getting them, but hadn't any proof. She seemed to think the marshal was covering up for him.

Two guys in this deal I hadn't yet met up with. One was Tailholt's manager, Bender. The other was her uncle who'd been running the works for her—Shellman Krole, whose sudden disappearance had brought her running to Cap.

I decided in the morning I'd have a talk with this guy, Bender.

What I most wanted now was a place to pound my ear. There were plenty of notions still prowling my mind but none of them appeared to have connection with Tailholt. The marshal was the only guy who'd mentioned the mine, and then only to point out I couldn't get a job there, or at the Signal Stope, Lucky Dog or Bell Clapper either.

I had just reached the end of the walk fronting Frunk's place when a girl's sudden scream pulled me out of my thinking. It had come out of the alley I was just about to cross, the passage stretching riverward between Frunk's Mercantile and the dark west side of the Eagle Hotel. It knifed, thinly frantic, through the sounds of raucous merriment, of fiddle-scrape and stamping boots pouring out of McCann's front doors.

A Ranger with any savvy, I reckon, would have done a heap of thinking before shoving his head in a hole like that. But not me. Not then. I yanked my gun and dived straight for the cry.

It was like jumping into a bottle of ink. I could scarcely see ten steps ahead of me but I could hear better now; I could hear a lot better. And I caught the pant of their ragged breathing, the scuffle and slap of struggling bodies.

I made them out when my eyes got to working. Not too good right at first but as a wild swaying blotch of heavier shadow against the black shapes of the trees beyond. He had her squeezed to him with an arm locked behind her. She wrenched away and broke free. But he had her again before she caught her balance, suddenly cursed, let her go and sprang away from her, wheeling.

I guessed what was coming and flung myself headlong. Even so, his blue whistler came almightly near getting me. It ripped through my hat with the sound of a hornet. I saw his gun flash again but I was already rolling. I came up through the echoes, not daring to fire on account of the girl —but it was all over now. She was running straight toward me and that sidewinding Short Creek was heating his axles, loping for the trees like a dog scairt rabbit.

Then the girl was beside me, pulling her torn blouse around her.

We stared at each other. We both cried *"You!"*

She laughed then, kind of shaky, and flung the tumble of hair back out of her eyes. "I'm sure thanking you," she panted, trying to keep herself covered. "You seem to be on hand every time I need help."

"Why's that whelp houndin' you?"

"Look!" She crouched, frightened. "There's someone else coming!"

That sharp, panicked edge to her words swung my head around. A pair of shapes from the street were moving into the passage.

The girl's hand, cold and trembly, caught hold on my arm. "Oh, please! Let's don't wait. I—"

One of the advancing pair growled, "What's the trouble back there?"

"No trouble," I said.

"Let's have a look at you."

The girl broke into a run. I ran after her. The other man bellowed, "Haul up or I'll fire!"

He fired; they both did. The whine of that lead was a spur to our efforts. We broke out of the alley, tore into the twice-as-dark gloom of the trees. The girl's hand swung me left. We pulled up and stood listening.

"They've quit," she decided. "Be careful with your feet now." Her hand pulled me toward the dark front of the hotel.

"Just a minute," I growled softly. "You blow out those lanterns?"

She shook her head.

I didn't like it. By the tone of her voice she didn't like it no better. "But we can't stand around out here all night," She said, "It's happened before."

"Were they out when you left the place?"

"I didn't think to notice. I went out the side door."

"To meet Short Creek?"

She didn't answer. She let go of my hand. I heard her move toward the verandah. Still scowling, I followed.

She stopped with a sudden harsh intake of breath.

A black shape had stepped from the gloom of the doorway. The hard bore of a gun dug into my stomach.

"That's fine. Stop right there," his voice told us; and:
"Gib—get a lamp lit. I've got him."

SEVEN

I HAD waltzed right into it like a bull with his eyes shut
And there wasn't one thing I could do about it, either—
not with Carolina standing right at my elbow.

He pulled the gun from my belt and dropped it in his
hip pocket. A light sprang up and wavered wild in the lobby.
abruptly steadied and turned yellow as the chimney was
snugged down into its sprockets. The guy motioned us in.

I followed the girl, marveling at the way she was keeping
her mouth shut. It came over me than I might have made
a mistake in not going straight to her and letting her know
Cap had sent me.

The lamp lighter, Gib, stood by the desk frowning at me
a cold-jawed bravo with a patch across one eye. I didn't
know him from Adam. I knew the other guy, though, the
one with the gun. It was the stoop-shouldered man in the
bullhide chaps, the sardine chewing redhead who had sat
on Frunk's counter.

His grin was not pleasant. There was a hard satisfaction in
the twist of his cheeks. "You wasn't lyin'. I'll say that for
you."

"Well . . . thanks."

"When you unloaded that brag about bein' so handy
But you showed damn pore judgment—your name's Tram
mell, ain't it?"

I said I reckoned it was.

He nodded. "This camp's pretty free but it ain't *that* free, bucko."

A vague disquiet began to pound at my bowels. "I'm slow to catch on," I said. "Chew it a little finer."

"You ready to gabble?"

"Gabble about what?"

"About who give you for instance the word to come down here."

"I didn't wait for no word. I go where there's money."

"You do for a fact," he said, scrinching his lips up. "Who give you the job?"

"What job?"

His narrowed eyes showed a glitter. "Set it up for him, Gib."

Eye Patch came over and dropped a hand on my shoulder. "You see this?" he said, and when I looked down I thought a mule had kicked me.

The next think I knew I was flopped in a chair. My shirt was wet. Water ran off my chin and the bucket in Gib's hand told me how it had got there.

"Stand up!" Rust Hair said. "Or do you wanta be helped?"

I climbed onto my feet. The room rocked around like a chip in a twister. When the girl and the rest of them quit floating past I reckoned I'd be able to keep down my supper.

"Who give you the job?"

We was back where we'd started. I groaned, put a hand up and gently felt of my jaw.

Rust Hair said, "It ain't busted yet. But it's goin' to be soon if you don't unlatch it."

I found the girl's face, "You know this feller?"

"Red Irick," she said—"one of Bucks Younger's deputies."

"And who is Bucks Younger?"

"The marshal of Shafts," Irick snorted. "Any more bright questions? Because if not, I'd admire to know what you two been doin' lopin' round in the dark."

I couldn't see anything wrong with telling him the truth,

but Carolina looked nervous. She tried to send me a message.

Irick caught her at it. "The gent's lost his tongue, Gib. See if you can find it."

Eye Patch grinned. He started rubbing his knuckles.

"Don't get excited," I said. "I'm going to tell you."

"Then start tellin'."

I gave it to him straight. The only thing I kept back was my hunch the guy was Short Creek.

"That the way you saw it?" Irick looked at Carolina.

"That's the way it *was*," she said, and looked right back at him.

"Maybe," Irick nodded, "an' then again, maybe not. How come you to be in that alley in the first place?"

"Is there any law against it?"

"Funny place for you to be." He dug a match from his pocket and jabbed a back tooth with it. He went over to the door and pushed it open and spat. Coming back he said abruptly, "Who you think jumped you?"

"It didn't get that far," she said, her cheeks crimson.

"Never mind bein' smart. You know what I mean. I want the guy's name."

The torn blouse, the way she held it, showed her breasts like they was naked.

I knew, all of a sudden, this was the question she'd been scared of. I could see it in her stare, the marble stiffness of her posture.

She finally made up her mind. "He didn't give me his name."

"Why didn't you stop when I hollered?"

"How was *I* to know it was you that hollered?" She fetched up her chin and her eyes came alive again. "I can't see in the dark any better than you can."

"You'd be surprised to know how good I can see. You're a cute little trick but don't push it too far. You was out in that passage all right, baby, but you wasn't out there with Trammell."

She kept her mouth shut.

I kept my lip buttoned, too. I couldn't figure what he was getting at or why so much seemed to hang on that alley. But I could see plain enough he knew more than he was telling.

And the same went for her.

"You want to tell me why you put them lanterns out?"

When she didn't answer that he took his hip off the desk. "Put your gun on this guy, Gib, while I look at his pistol."

He got it out of his pocket, shook the loads out and counted them. Then he held it to his nose and took a sniff of the barrel, nodding. "Smart," he said, and showed a grudging admiration. "You're a slicker piece of goods than anyone around here figured. So maybe you'll get away with it."

He walked up to me. "You've got a lot of nerve, Trammell. You better make the most of it. You can start by tellin' who you done the job for."

I hadn't done any job so I didn't say anything. He didn't, either.

WHEN I came round again I was soaking. I didn't care about that—it was the blood that really got me. It was in my mouth and all over my shirt and my face felt like the whole front was caved in. Staring up from the horror of my own spilled gore I could see the lips moving in the girl's stormy face and Irick glaring like a prodded steer and, back of him, Eye Patch with his dripping bucket.

Which was when I caught sight of my gun in Irick's fist. I had to see the light flashing off its seven-inch barrel before I understood why I wasn't standing up there with them.

I commenced to hear sound, feeble at first but very swiftly growing louder till it hit the full bellow of Irick's shouted roar. "Never mind the goddam bucket! Get him on his feet I said!"

Eye Patch's chest floated over me. I felt his hands go under me. He sucked in a great breath and I came off the floor with the room spinning round my head like a rope. My shoulderblades bumped and with a sickening suddenness the

walls latched onto their foundations and froze there. I was
propped against one of them, held in position by Eye Patch's
strength till some of the sag got out of my knee joints.

Irick shoved him aside with his look dark and ugly.

"I'm all through foolin'," he said, grating each word like it
was nuts he was cracking. "You come clean an' come quick
or I'll ram that goddam gun down your throat!"

I opened my mouth, but no words came out.

"Your name's Trammell, ain't it?"

I croaked assent.

"You got room Number Nine?"

"I ain't got *any* room yet. I'm—"

"Don't give me that! Your name's in the—"

"But all the rooms was filled up! This guy in Number
Nine—"

"What guy?"

"Crafkin."

Irick looked at Gib. Gib trotted to the desk. "No Crafkin
in the book—"

"But there *must* be," I said. "I talked to the feller—"

"The point," Irick growled, "is that you've got the room
now."

"I ain't been near the damn room!"

"Then what's your gear doin' in it? Your shotgun, rifle an'
bedroll," Irick sneered—"an' don't tell me they ain't in it
because we've already seen them."

"I can't help that. Crafkin—"

"I've had enough of your run-around!" Irick slammed
me against the wall. "Search 'im, Gib."

Eye Patch said, hauling his hand from my pocket, "Is
this what we're lookin' for?" and held up a key. The 9 on
the tag looked big as a house.

Irick's look turned ugly. "Never been near the room, eh?"

I licked the blood off my lips. "Of course I've got the
key. I told you Crafkin—"

"There ain't no Crafkin—"

"Ask the girl," I said. "She'll tell you!"

Carolina looked surprised. "We've had no guest of that name."

"What!" I said, not believing my ears. "That cattle buyer! That feller that piled off the stairs onto——"

"You must be mistaken." She looked completely bewildered. "We haven't any cattle buyer staying at this hotel. The last guest we had in Number Nine was Krentz, the condiments and spice man. The room wasn't occupied when you signed for it."

I guess I stared like a fool. I got cold all over when Irick touched my shoulder. I said through chattering teeth, "What's the matter with the room?"

"I'm goin' to show you, Handy. An' maybe while you're lookin' you can tell us why you killed him."

"Killed who?" the girl cried.

"Why, your uncle. Shellman Krole."

EIGHT

I HAD plenty of time to think things over after Irick locked me up in the one-room adobe which served as Shafts' official juzgado. It was not an imposing edifice but its walls were twenty-four inches thick and its single window, covered with half-inch screening, backed up by a row of two-inch pipes. It contained no furnishings save a thin pile of oat straw intended for a bed and, in the opposite corner, a little pile of sand which might serve the needs of nature. There was twelve feet of empty space between roof and floor and the door was made of two-inch planks secured by a mas-

sive padlock. Nothing short of an Act of God could get a
man loose without outside help.

These things I had seen by the light of his lantern which
Irick had thoughtfully taken away with him. My untended
face was giving me hell and my thoughts weren't anything
to brag about, either. I had sure wound up in one beautiful
mess for a guy that was going to be a second Burt Mossman.

I couldn't understand that girl at all. But there were
other things, too—like why were they going to so much
trouble with me when a slug through the back would have
stopped me permanent, not to mention being easier and
quicker.

The only reasonable answer was that they knew or suspected I had come from Cap Murphey. But didn't the fools
know he'd send another Ranger up here if the first one he
sent got put out of business?

The pain in my head wasn't helping me think, but I did
pull one notion out of the tangle. What happened to me
might not bother them any so long as I was stopped and so
long as what happened to me couldn't be laid to the mind
that had planned it. This might logically explain the slick
way I'd been framed for the killing of a man who must
have stood in their way. Shellman Krole, according to the
dope Cap had passed along to me, had been undertaking to
show a profit from the various holdings of the Tailholt Mining & Milling Company which belonged, I understood, to
Carolina Krole. The hotel wasn't hers and the milling end
of the business, so far as I knew, was doing all right. It
was the mining end of the venture, and Shellman Krole's
disappearance, which had brought the girl into Cap Murphey's office.

Krole, according to her tell of it, had disappeared between mine and town two days before she had yelled for a
Ranger. And now he was dead with two slugs in his back
and killed, to my thinking, not more than half an hour before I'd clapped eyes on him. Where had he been in the

meantime, and what in the world had he been doing in Number Nine?

It seemed obvious to me he must have stumbled on something, been discovered in his discovery and taken out of circulation before he could pass the good word along. He had not been nice to look at when Irick had choused us up there to see him. But the girl hadn't fainted. She hadn't sobbed. She hadn't opened her mouth. For all her expression had revealed to the contrary she might have been looking at a piece of waste paper.

It wasn't natural.

It wasn't natural, either, for the sleeves of Krole's shirt to be wrinkled like they were just above both elbows.

There was a heap of unnatural things in this deal, including those blown-out lanterns. Who'd blown them out? Carolina? Or Irick? And what was the object? To conceal what was going on back in that alley?

No one seemed to know exactly what *had* been going on. Except, of course, the girl; and she wasn't talking. Like Irick, I was curious to know what she'd been doing out there in the first place. A funny place for her to be, Red Irick had said; and I thought so, too. Considering time and location I thought it damned queer.

It was a devil of a lot queerer the way she had cut the ground out from under me by denying the existence of that cattle buyer, Crafkin. What the hell had she thought to gain by that? Did she think I was dumb enough to swallow that garble? Or that I wouldn't remember him? Or, knowing already what was in store for me—But, if she had known that much, she must also have known what had happened to her uncle; and if she had known that . . .

I shook my head, and wished immediately I hadn't for it started my face to hurting full tilt again. If I ever got the chance, I promised myself, I was going to show Irick what a pistoling felt like. With interest.

I walked up and down the cramped confines of my prison, thoughts whirling. Piece by piece I went over the things I had seen or heard since I'd run into Irick on the hotel verandah. But they didn't add up. There was too much missing. Maybe I was just a handy goat, but I felt in my bones I'd been deliberately framed by someone my presence had embarrassed or frightened.

It had to be someone who was mixed up with Tailholt, else there'd been no point in killing Shellman Krole. Was it Gharst or the marshal? Was it Frunk or the girl? And what about Short Creek—where did he fit into this?

I was damn near certain it had to be one of them. One of five people. But which one was it?

A stealthy sound spun my face to the window. It was lighter outside, but not very much.

Very carefully and slowly I got down on my knees, never taking my eyes from that glassless window. There was someone out there, someone being mighty cautious.

I didn't think it would be any of the bunch who had framed me. But it might be the one who'd buried that blade in Gharst's door.

I hardly dared breathe lest the sidewinder hear me.

Then a voice crept softly in through the window. "Trammell?"

Ever try to peg the person back of a whisper?

I waited, heart pounding.

The screen might keep a knife from whipping in through that opening but it wouldn't stop a bullet.

"Trammell? Are you there? This is Carolina."

Maybe it was. And maybe it wasn't. I didn't say a word.

"Listen—where are you? I'm going to get you out of there. There's an ore wagon up the street—I'm going to drive it down here. I'll slip a chain around those bars and yank out the window. I've tied a horse at the corner. Be ready to run for it."

I didn't know what to think hardly.

It might actually be here. I couldn't tell without moving. The whole thing could be a trick.

A lot of questions plagued my mind but I didn't let them plague me into moving or talking.

One thing I felt reasonably sure of. It was her had got

me into this. If I hadn't dashed into that alley to help her I wouldn't have been with her when she reached that dark verandah. If she hadn't lied about Crafkin I probably wouldn't have been in this calaboose. I remembered something then, something Irick had said right after he'd sniffed of my gun barrel. "Smart," he had said with a kind of grudging admiration. "You're a slicker piece of goods than anyone around here figured." I had supposed at the time he had intended those words for me. Now I wasn't so sure.

But say the whisperer was Carolina. Was it because she had helped put me into this jail that she had come around now with this stunt to get me out of it? Remorse? A guilty conscience? I didn't think a girl who could lie the way she had could have enough conscience to worry about. But she might have plenty of reasons for wanting me out of this camp, I thought.

And that was another thing. Trap or no trap, if I left by that window I'd be laying myself open to the slug of any guy that wanted to take a shot at me—a fugitive, wanted for the killing of Shellman Krole.

I got onto my feet and edged across to the window. I didn't see any lurkers waiting round in the shadows. Across the dark open stretch of the unpaved street I could see a lone light in the stage depot office. It was the only light showing now in Canada Gulch.

I tried to scout out the corner where she'd left the tied horse but there weren't any corners in sight from the window. I didn't see any tied horses, either.

I wondered what Burt Mossman would have done in my place, but that didn't help because I couldn't imagine Mossman being caught in such a trap.

I was sure in one hell of a spot for a Ranger!

I guessed I would just have to take my chances and go through that window no matter what happened afterwards.

I had just reached that conclusion when I heard the crunch of booted feet outside. These weren't stealthy steps; they came straight up to the door. I caught the rattle of the hasp

and the sound of someone's key thrusting into the padlock,
and I thought: *That goddam Irick again.*

But it wasn't Red Irick. I knew that much before the
door opened, when the guy outside said, "Trammell? Stand
in front of the window. I'm coming in for a talk."

It was the marshal, Bucks Younger, and he had come without a lantern.

I didn't know what that signified, but he had sure picked
a first class time to come calling. With the girl probably
driving up the street right now.

I reckoned Murphey was right about me and savvy. If
I'd had enough sense to pound sand down a rat hole I would
probably have come up with some fine inspiration that would
have knocked all my problems into a cocked hat. But if I'd
had that much sense I wouldn't have been in this jailhouse.

All I could think of to say was "Okay."

"Get over there then and don't be trying any tricks."

He was too alert to be taken in by anything conjured on
the spur of the moment. He remained where he was until
I'd crossed the room. He came in then, still holding the
padlock, and put his broad back against the closed door.

"It will save time," he said, "if I tell you at once she's
not coming with that wagon without it suits my book."

In the gloom of this room I could not see his expression.
I was just as well pleased to know he couldn't see mine.
"What do you want?"

"I want to know first of all if you killed Shellman Krole."

"How could I kill a man I hadn't ever seen?"

"We haven't time to spar around. I want a straight answer. Did you or didn't you?"

"No. I did not."

"What did you think of Brian Gharst?"

I stared at him tightly. "Any guy as thorough as you are
hadn't ought to have to ask!"

"I regret the necessity. It's unfortunate I can't be two
places at once, but there it is. I can't quite make myself in-
visible. either. What did you think of him?"

"I didn't like him," I said. "Did you throw that knife?"

I caught the faint sound of his insucked breath. "Maybe you had better tell me about that."

I told him.

"*Someone*," he said, "doesn't want you around."

I said, "I'm beginnin' to be of that opinion myself."

"What did you think of Gideon Frunk?"

"I wouldn't care to eat off the same plate with him."

"There's bad blood shaping up between him and Gharst. They've been sniping at each other for quite a while now. I suppose Gharst wanted you to spy on Frunk."

"That seemed to be the general notion."

Younger nodded. "I've an idea Frunk's getting fed up with Gharst's interference. He's got the upper hand right now and means to keep it." He looked at me earnestly. At least, his voice sounded earnest when he said in that quiet direct way that seemed to characterize all of his more serious remarks. "I'd like to help you, Trammell. You're in a bad spot here. I'm in a bad spot myself and I believe you could help me. I think it would be smart for us to put our heads together."

Riding a hunch, I said: "What do you think of Carolina?"

"She's playing with matches," he said thoughtfully. "I haven't had much chance to know her personally. The disappearance of her uncle, following so closely on the heels of her father's death, has kind of started her running in circles. She's convinced someone's trying to beat her out of her mine, and she has some reason for thinking so. Unfortunately she's stubborn, given to making snap judgments and entirely too brash where she ought to be cautious."

"Just how do you mean?"

"Well, for one thing, she's determined to get to the bottom of the business. But she won't let me help her—she won't let me near the place. She thinks Frunk's grabbing her concentrates and, for some crazy reason, she's got the idea I'm helping him."

"You said she was playing with matches."

Younger said gruffly, "She's playing with something a lot more dangerous than matches. In her desire to get to the

bottom of this business, she's made some kind of deal with the
wrong kind of people. I assume she has, anyway, because
she's smart enough to know she would have to have help.
Obviously she wouldn't go to Frunk and she hasn't come to
me."

"You think she's gone to Gharst?"

"I don't know. The Tailholt's the richest mine in these
diggings—I'm pretty well satisfied of that. Like Carolina,
I don't believe her father's death was due to any accident,
though it certainly was made to look like one. Just between
you and me, I wouldn't be astonished to learn that Carolina's
mine is the real direct cause of the feud that's sprang up
between Gharst and Frunk."

"You think they're both after it?"

"I think it's quite likely."

"You got any reasons?"

"Nothing I could put a finger on."

"Either one offered to buy her out?"

"I don't know about Gharst. Frunk made her an offer."

"How much?"

"He is reported to have offered fifty thousand."

"You think it's worth more?"

"Your guess is as good as mine," Younger said. "I have
never known Frunk to offer a quarter of what anything was
worth."

I told him about Frunk's purchase of Roy's hole and he
sighed. "That's his system, all right. First scare the guy
and then buy him out cheap. He's done that before."

"You think he's trying to scare the girl?"

"She's already scared. She's got more backbone than the
rest of this bunch Frunk has put pressure on. She's trying
to fight back. I think he's playing a freeze-out game. I don't
say he's getting her concentrates, but she can't get the stuff
to market. She's having trouble underground. She hasn't
got much money. I think whoever is behind what's going on
is trying to tie her up so tight she'll simply *have* to sell out"

"You think they could do that?"

"I believe that thought is behind present tactics."

"And there's nothing you can do?"

"That remains to be seen. I think I might be able to do something about it if I could manage to find out what's really going on. I can't do much working solely on rumor. She won't let me near the place. She's got a fence around the diggings patrolled by eight men with rifles."

"What about the help? You can't get out ore without miners."

"They're only working three men. And Jeff Bender, of course, the mine manager."

Still riding my hunch, I told him about Brian Gharst's proposition.

"About what I figured," Younger answered. "You won't get much change out of Gideon Frunk. His organization's all set; he wouldn't risk taking on new blood now."

"Your deputy, Irick, seems on good terms with him."

Younger laughed shortly. "He ought to be," he said. "It was Frunk that had Red Irick made deputy."

"Frunk told me," I said, "to ask you for a job."

"Knowing, of course, that if I gave you one he could knock it in the head by having his Better Business Bureau refuse to vote any pay for you."

I thought that over. I said, "What about the job you offered me yourself?"

"I didn't plan to advertise that you were a deputy. It was an undercover job that I was figuring to give you. I was aiming to pay you out of what I'm paid myself."

He stood quiet a moment, thinking. "That's why I'm over here now. When I found out the girl was going to try to break you out of here I got the driver of that wagon to stick around it for awhile."

"What do you want me to do?" I said.

"I want to get you into that mine. If she pulls you out of this place she's going to figure—"

"It won't work," I said, and told him of the conversations which had led up to my being here; of how Irick had got the drop on me and of how the girl had denied the whole existence of Crafkin. "All she wants," I said, "is to see the

last of me. She wants to get me out of the country and figures
I'll be glad to get out if she gives me half a chance."

"Thinking, of course, you're the only one who can tie her
up with that cattle buyer."

"If he *is* a cattle buyer, which I'm beginning to doubt."

"No cattle buyer of his description has ever been through
here before. Something odd, too, about him not being regis-
tered. I expect we can pretty safely conclude he's some new
man she's got working for her. Some fellow she wants to keep
out of sight. She obviously has no reason for believing you
connected with her uncle's death or she wouldn't be trying
to get you out of here. I think if you'd work at it a little you
could get her to hire you."

"You mean you're willing to turn me loose?"

"I'm a pretty good judge of human nature," he said dryly. "You don't look to me like the kind of a gent that would
shoot another man through the back. I've got to get somebody into that mine before it's too late to do her any good.
This mysterious Crafkin convinces me I was on the right
track in thinking she was getting in over her head. If she's
hired one tough character, I see no real reason why she
wouldn't hire another—meaning you. But it will be damned
risky. You'll have to watch your step every minute of the
time. In addition to that, if you let her snake you out of
here, I can't give you any protection. Red Irick will be
howling for your scalp soon's he sees that jerked-out window.
Frunk will probably post a reward for you and—"

"I'm willing to take my chances," I said. "You don't think
Carolina killed her uncle herself, do you—or had him
killed?"

Younger said sharply, "Where'd you get that notion?"

"Irick seemed to think—"

"Irick," Younger said, "thinks whatever Frunk wants
him to."

NINE

'I'M SORRY I was so long," she whispered, "but we're all set now. I couldn't find anything to cut that screen; you'll just have to pray that when this chain jerks these bars it will pull the whole works out. Irick went off with your pistol and I couldn't find your rifle. But that sawed-off's on your saddle and your horse is tied just around the corner, between here and the assayer's—next building to your left. Are you ready?"

"Been mighty good of you to go to all—"

"You've got that much coming."

"I hope you won't get in no—"

"Never mind me! Listen to what I'm telling you. When this window comes out you come right out after it—don't stop for anything! Pile right into your saddle and give that pony everything you've got."

I reckoned she wasn't going to like any part of this and, as she slipped off into the roundabout shadows, it came into my mind I might not like it much either when the whole hand was down. If she was tricking me again, or if somebody else was, I might easy wind up to be a mighty dead duck. Especially if that horse wasn't where she said it was.

All kind of wild thoughts was rushing through my head—not to mention the pain from my face, which was plenty. I was a lone white chip in a no-limit game and I had no guarantee that even Younger was backing me.

But a guy has to put a little faith in something and, like Bucks had said, we had one thing in our favor; nobody'd be looking for me to be on the payroll of a galoot I'd knocked around the way I had Bucks Younger.

I could see the shapes of the waiting horses, three pairs of them, hitched to the front of that wagon. The high bulk

of that rig was not ten feet from the window. I hoped nobody wondered what the hell it was doing there. Probably
they wouldn't. So far as I could see, this whole street was
dark, no saloons or honkytonks on it except for Jawbone
Clark's dancehall, next door to the right, about eighty feet
away and not doing no business anyway.

And right then was when that struck me as peculiar, but
I didn't get no chance to think about it because just at that
moment I saw the girl's shape climb onto the seat and un-
wrap the lines.

I heard her cluck to the horses, saw them take up the
slack and move into their collars. Then the whip popped
over their heads and they dug into it, the great wheels turning, the chain clanking tight.

One moment that window was where it had always been;
the next it was gone, pipes screen and all, in a great cloud
of dust. I didn't wait around for any probable results. I
went out through the dust of that wrecked wall running.

The horse was right there where she had said he would be,
and right alongside of him a guy with his gun out.

I had to look twice because the shadows were thicker
than blue tail flies, but I could see enough of him to make
damn sure he wasn't cached out there to give me any hand
up.

It was that bony faced kid—that sidewinding Short
Creek!

I made a wild dive just ahead of the flash, then a jump
to the right and a quick lunge left again, wondering how
long I'd keep ahead of his bullets. I'd bid goodbye to the
horse fast as ever I'd seen him and was bending all my
efforts towards getting around that corner where the whipped
pine planking of the assayer's office would be between me
and that vinegarroon's pistol.

I was bent nearly double and barely inches from my
objective when a rolling bottle flung me off my balance.
I went through the air like a bird and lit rolling, expecting
any moment I would draw my last breath. But the fool
had shot his gun plumb dry and before he could get it to

banging again I was up on my feet and round the side of the building.

I didn't stop to write no letters.

The black wall of the gulch was straight before me. I couldn't tell how steep it was or anything else. I just tore into it and went scrabbling upward fast as I could catch holds to grab onto.

I was almost to the rim when the first of a bunch of gun-waving jaspers came pounding around the corner of that shack and froze me against that wall like a possum. Long as I wasn't skylined I knew that bunch couldn't see me. But I was in a tough spot with one foot half lifted and about to change hands. I was scared to go on and scared even more to set the foot down lest it dislodge a rock and draw a bedlam of gunfire. I clung like grim death and prayed that nothing would tear loose.

I couldn't see much but I could hear the low buzz of their excited mutterings. To the south and east I could smell the damp cold of the river, the scorched odor of dust churned up by their boots as they went nosing around like a pack of stumped curs. Then one guy said plainly, "Mebbe he went up the cliff," and I could feel the stab of their searching eyes.

Somebody scoffed. "In this dark? No one but a dimwit like you would—"

Irick's punishing voice lunged through it. "You goin' to stand there all night? Spread out an' beat the bushes! Couple of you tackle that cliff! Rest of you split up an' comb both sides of these buildin's—by God, I want that walloper caught!"

I could hear them spreading out, breaking up and moving off, and with an increasing clarity I could hear a pair of them somewhere beneath me moving through the brush around the base of the cliff. "Hell," one of them said, "he never went up there. That's a bad enough place to try to scale in the daytime. With all that loose shale we'd of heard him sure."

"Yeah, but you heard Red. He said to go up."

"That guy says a lot of things besides his prayers."

"He's damn quick on the trigger, too, an' don't you forget it."

"What'd this feller do, anyway?"

"Busted outa the jail—"

"I mean before. What'd they put him in for?"

"How the hell would I know? You think I—"

The blast of a gun cut through their talk, followed almost at once by three further shots.

I knew what that was. They were potshotting shadows.

But the pair down beneath me seemed to have froze in their tracks. You could almost feel their bated breath. "Hell's fire!" one cried, and the other guy yelled, "C'mon—they've got him!" and went crashing off through the breaking brush.

I couldn't tell if they both went or not. I didn't wait to find out. I went over that cliff like a bat out of Carlsbad.

It wasn't near so dark up here as down yonder where the plain-to-view lights of the camp's main drag made every shadow look twice as black. But it was still too dark to go ramming around at the top of your whistle. Soon as I judged I was away from the rim I stopped to catch breath and get my bearings.

I wasn't out of this yet. All I had done was swap jail for the open. I might, in fact, have swapped the witch for the devil. I didn't have no horse. I was on my own without a gun in country I didn't know anything about, pitting my wits against a bunch of tough rannies who could find their way around with their eyes shut. The same bunch probably which had snuffed Krole's light. And would be glad to snuff mine, given half a chance.

If I went straight ahead I reckoned I'd come out someplace just a little beyond the uninhabited end of Burro Alley, somewhere around that little red schoolhouse I had noticed while riding into this camp. That might make me a hideout for the next two-three hours but, when school took up, I would have to move again.

It looked like being a lot smarter to do my moving now.

I started forward slow, feeling my way and keeping my

ears skinned. If anybody and me was going to meet up here it was my intention to be the first one to know it.

This ground all lay pretty level in a kind of rolling bench sloping gently as I walked and spotted here and there with occatilla and greasewood and the occasional dark shape of a twisted catclaw. A few trees stood starkly limned against the glow from below, but nothing showed this bench was ever used by anybody. All the digging, it seemed like, was on the far side of town.

I thought the best place to hide would be that room in the hotel where they had found Shellman Krole. That seemed the one sure place where I would not be looked for.

I even managed to figure out how I could get there. By skirting the west end of Burro Alley and heading straight south beyond the town limits I could reach the river. Its near bank was grown to cottonwoods and willows and, by keeping to the water and using a little care, I figured I could leave it right in front of the hotel. If those lanterns were still out I could go right on up.

The prospect of a bed, even shared with a corpse, if they hadn't moved him out yet, looked a heap more inviting to me right now than any other prospect I could think of. I was pretty near ready to drop in my tracks. Nothing but the knowledge of what would happen if they found me was preventing me from dropping down and snoozing right up here.

I wondered how much Irick was offering for my scalp.

I got to thinking then of Crafkin, the elusive tenant of room Number Nine whom that girl had never seen or even so much as heard of—to hear her tell the story. He *had* had that room because it was him that had given me the key to it. Had Krole been in there then? Was Crafkin the guy who had killed him? Why had Carolina denied his existence? What was between Carolina Krole and Crafkin?

There were pleny of questions prowling through my head, and one other thing. The thought of Cap Murphey. It was that trouble at Tailholt that had fetched me up here, and Tailholt was where I'd ought to be right now.

I had been in this camp going on nine hours and hadn't
even got within gunshot of it. I had lost my horse and all
my artillery and was being hunted now for the killing of
the man who had been in charge of Tailholt. I could see
what Cap had meant about savvy.

What I'd ought to do was get into that mine—but how
could I? How was I going to get through that fence? And
the nine men with rifles that was being paid to watch it?
I could try, of course; but my best bet, it looked like, was
to talk that girl into hiring me. And the best place to find
her was at the Eagle Hotel.

The ground underfoot was slanting a lot more noticeable
and I reckoned I was getting pretty close to where this
bench angled down toward the schoolhouse. I'd have to
keep my eyes peeled. With those Burro Alley cribs still doing
a lively business—

Right then was where I stopped, with the toe of one boot
shoved into something that was yielding horribly under my
weight. I jumped back away from it, bathed in sweat.

All the sounds of the night stepped up their rustlings and
the breeze coming out of the gulch blew colder.

I dropped onto my knees and, knowing the full folly of it,
rasped a match on my Levis and watched its cupped flare
ravel through the layered gloom to wash its oil-yellow shine
across the shape of fat Roy. He lay sprawled on his back and
he was dead as a doornail.

TEN

I PUT out the match and rocked back on my bootheels,
stomach muscles crawling in the dread expectation of hearing the cry that must tell of my discovery.

But nothing happened. No cry came, no bullet.

The rustling quiet disclosed no change, yet I was not fooled into thinking I was safe. Somewhere in this night men with loaded guns were hunting me, prowling the backs of buildings, overturning packing crates, peering into all the dark and hidden places—perhaps, even now, they were beating both banks of the river.

I didn't have to see Roy's face again to know he had not died peacefully. Someone had beaten the back of his head in. There was no sign of a weapon on him.

I was beginning to feel kind of dizzy. I knew I had got to get some rest before the shakes in my legs let me down completely. I didn't like to leave Roy laying there but to be caught near him by Irick would be all those birds was needing to fit a hemp necktie around my neck.

I got onto my feet and started back upslope. I'd give up my notion of trying to get to the river. I was scared to cross that Burro Gulch trail lest I be seen and later accused of Roy's killing. It was in my mind maybe Irick had done it for those fifty silver dollars. Or on Frunk's instructions. Either way, if he had (or if he knew about it even), there was a mighty good chance he was having the body watched.

My aching face was giving me hell and my thoughts wasn't calculated to cheer me much, neither. Any way I turned I seemed to get in deeper; and right about then I began to wonder if the most of this grief hadn't come right out of my trying to play gumshoe without no experience. It wasn't my style in the first place and I was pretty well convinced by now in my own mind that the only damn polecat I was fooling was me.

THEY hadn't moved my horse.

That was one blessing, anyway.

He was still standing hipshot right where Carolina had tied him. Where I lay on the rim above that pine plank assayer's shack I had an unbothered view of him and I watched him

ten minutes and all those roundabout shadows without seeing anything that looked at all suspicious.

I reckoned Irick's hunt had moved to likelier locations.

I eased myself across the rim and started down the cliff
cautious. I didn't want to bump into trouble before I reached
that horse.

I took my time, resting every couple of yards or so, and
when I got to the bottom I stood quiet awhile, listening. The
only thing I could hear was the fitful coughing of that chilly
wind.

I didn't aim to make any more mistakes. I worked my
way through the brush with a dogged, watchful patience.
Coming out of it I moved into the deeper shadows of the
pine plank shack where I stayed a long ten minutes, storing
up strength and finding out all the night had to tell me. When
I judged there was no cause for any further alarm I got on
my feet again and started for my horse.

It would feel powerful good, I thought, to get a saddle
under me.

My mind was made up now. I was done with caution. I
was all through ducking and dodging. I aimed to learn these
dadblamed crooks around here that a Arizona Ranger was
no guy to yell *boo!* at.

About twenty feet ahead was the corner around which I
had so desperately dashed a half hour ago trying to get
out of reach of that Short Creek's pistol. A little ways beyond
the corner was my waiting horse and there was going to
be a new deal quick as I could get my legs around his
barrel. It might not be any better deal but it was damn
sure going to be a different one.

Rounding that corner I got the surprise of my life. A gun
went off practically right in my face. Unhit but half blinded I tore into the guy swinging. He never had no chance to
squeeze his trigger again. My lifted right knee caught him
flush in the groin and as it doubled him forward a gorgeous
left hook almost unhinged his jaw.

It spun him half around but I could see a lot better now.
I got him by the coat collar, swung him quick and wide and

let him go crashing up against that plank wall. The gun fell out of his fist with a clatter. As he sagged I went after it.

I was bent over, trying to reach it, when I saw his boot turn. I got back just in time. The down-flashing glint of that murderous blade didn't miss my cheek by the thinnest of whiskers. I struck out at him wildly. tried to whirl but he tripped me. His weight slammed into me.

I plowed through the dust on a hip and one shoulder. He came down on my legs but I rolled, twisting free before he could skewer me.

He was onto his feet almost quick as I was, panting and snarling, coming right after me. It was hard to keep track of that hand in these shadows. Always it was there, scarcely inches away, a confused weaving blur of thrusting and slashing in its continual endeavor to sheathe that steel in my body.

I had to keep giving ground. I had to keep my arms clear. On this uneven footing, with those spurs on my heels, I was in an agony of terror lest I get hung up or stumble. I was scared even more of turning my back on him.

But there's an end—even to nightmares. This one ended with the small of my back jammed into a tie rail. I saw the shine of his teeth, saw his hand go up. Then he gathered himself and came at me full tilt.

At the very last moment I lifted a leg up. My boot caught him flush in the chest, drove him backward. He was still off balance when my left fist buried itself in his belly. But his damned knife got me.

It got me high in the back. I could feel it lay open my flesh to the bone. I could feel the hot flow of my cascading blood.

The guy was down but by the sounds he was making he was figuring to get up again. I watched him come over onto hands and knees. I heard him groan. I saw him back around like a beak-pinched grasshopper and, after canting his head a couple times, start moving.

He still had the knife. I could see the dull glint of its blade as he crawled toward me. I didn't wait for him to reach me. He had the knife in his right hand and I kicked that wrist as hard as I could. He screamed like a dying horse. He quit when I kicked him in the face and I thought the sound of those breaking teeth was the sweetest music I had heard in a coon's age.

I had a hard time finding the tie rack. I thought I never would get the knot out of those reins. And when I did the damn horse acted like he didn't know me, snorting and shying round like a bronc with a cockleburr under his blankets. I don't know how I got my foot in the stirrup or how long it took me to get into the saddle or what the hell I planned to do after. I remember breaking my Greener to make sure it was loaded and the night kind of fogging up like smoke.

The next thing I knew I was flat on my back in a bed staring up at a lamp lighted ceiling.

I GOT to know that ceiling like the palm of my hand before I was able to get out of that bed. I knew every crack in it—every knothole. I didn't know whose drawers I was in but they were too loose to be mine. The guy must have a whole raft of them because I'd been here two weeks and every day they got changed by the girl who sang in the Bellyful Bar.

It had taken me some time to recall who she was but on my fourth awakening to full consciousness I pegged her. There was no forgetting such feline grace, that tremendous vitality so apparent in every gesture—those eyes. Though everything about her was of of an amazing loveliness it was her eyes that a man would most certainly remember. Tawny, they were, and indescribably female, at once so wise and yet so childlike, so sad yet so eager—like sunlight rocking across windrowed sand in the first flush of morning. Purely golden.

Soledad, they called her.

That song I had first heard her singing—*Jalisco*—was as truly her as anything I can think of. Like a drumbeat, like the clickety-clack of castanets; the rattle of musketry before a white wall. What words can reveal her? The total impression was not a thing of the features; like the willowy sight of her breath-taking body these were perfection. Can you describe the essence of wind or flame? Or tie a string to the moon?

No more can I tell you what Soledad looked like.

Her living flesh, yes. I could tell you of that. I could tell you her lips were the color of crushed berries, her nose without flaw, her skin like old ivory, her eyes deep pools wherein a man could willingly lose even honor—yet you would not know her. Words are too easily mouthed, too flat, too threadbare with use to recapture her image. There is nothing to which I could compare her that would make you see her as I did. You would not guess the knife-twisting tenderness of her. Your skin would not tingle to her smile as mine did nor your heart bound as mine to the touch of her fingers.

She was the plaything of moods, unpredictable, distracting. Caring nothing for convention she had her own code of rules and was, in her way, devoutly religious.

I remember the morning of my fourth awakening. Returning just short of dawn from a night's tour of earning her keep among Gharst's boisterous patrons, she found my eyes sensible of her presence and came at once to my side, dropping a cool hand to my forehead. "You are better," she smiled. "You will mend now, quickly. Ah, *pobrecito*—I am glad for you. The Blessed Virgin be praised. It was a near thing, that."

She ran the cool hand over my whiskery cheek. "You are hungry."

She went back of the bed then beyond my view. I heard the rustle and swish of discarded clothing, the clatter of kicked-off spike-heeled shoes. I heard her bare feet cross the pine boards of the flooring, more slithering cloth and she came into sight in fresh gingham, arms twisted back of her, buttoning it up.

I watched her thrust shapely feet into scuffed huaraches, get her purse from a battered old chest of drawers.

I dozed off then. When next I opened my eyes she was beside me, on the floor with a bowl of steaming broth. "You must eat," she explained, and proceeded to feed me. It was good—to the very last drop it was good. I could feel strength's return flowing into my arteries.

The next time I woke she was in bed with me, sleeping. And the whiskers, I found, were gone from my face.

She was right. I commenced to mend rapidly. My curiosity grew apace. By the end of my eighth day in that room I was fed to the gills with being so useless and, after she'd left, attempted to get up. I did get up—at least I got my feet on the floor. I was glad enough to lie down again quick. I was not as recovered as I had liked to imagine.

During the next couple of days I did a great deal of thinking. I asked Soledad what talk she had heard about my sudden disappearance.

"It is thought you have gone, run away," she smiled. "Already you have been forgotten, *mi alma*. Have no worry, we have been at much trouble that no on should guess where you are."

"We?"

"Certainly. Did you think I could get you up here by myself? The Señor Gharst and Pete Spence brought you here between them."

I had thought it very likely Gharst had known I was here. Remembering his words I was surprised he had bothered.

I wondered what Bucks Younger was thinking. Had he known I was a Ranger when he made me his deputy? Someone had known, of that much I felt certain. Either the girl had been followed when she'd gone to Cap Murphey or she'd made the mistake of confiding in someone. I wondered if Gharst knew.

I thought probably they all did by this time. I'd concealed my badge in the skirt of my saddle, between the leather and the lining. I asked Soledad if she knew what had happened to my horse. She said the marshal had him.

I considered Carolina. I still couldn't figure why she'd denied knowing Crafkin unless Younger had the right of it in thinking the fellow was some gun-slinger she had fetched in here to help her unravel what was happening at Tailholt. Perhaps that was where he had gone that night with some kind of password that would get him through the fence.

I recalled Irick's talk again, his veiled suggestion that Carolina might know more about what had happened to her uncle than was apparent. I could not believe she'd had a hand in killing him—it was against all reason. And yet, why had she been out in that alley? And how had Short Creek known he would find her there? Who had put out those lanterns that were hung from the roof of the Eagle's verandah?

I asked Soledad if she knew Short Creek.

She thought it over awhile and then nodded. "He is bad, that one—*hombre malo.*"

Pressed for reasons, all she would say was that he was understood to have killed several men. She tossed back her hair and regarded me sullenly. "If we must waste time in talk let us talk of ourselves." Kicking off her huaraches she came and sat on the bed. "I would lay with you if you asked me."

"You lay with me half the day," I said gruffly, but she brushed that aside.

"To sleep!" she said scornfully. "Am I then so ugly?" She held up a leg, letting her skirt fall away. "Is it crooked? Here—feel with your hand. Is it rough?"

"It's all right," I said without touching it.

She glared. "What's the matter with you?"

"With that hole in my back I don't—"

"Ah, *pobrecito!*" She swung up her legs, twisted around and put her lips against mine. I thought she'd never let go. I would lie if I said she did not excite me, but as soon as I could I tore loose and rolled over. She came after me, twisting her mouth into mine, hotly, hungrily, straining against me.

I could feel the pound of her heart against mine. Maybe I was too weak for it. She drew back of a sudden and looked at me angrily. "You're afraid!"

I was. Just a little. I was afraid this might be some trick of Brian Gharst's. After all, he knew where I was, and where she was.

I said, "I think right now we'd be smarter to talk."

"About . . . us?"

"And other things. How do you come to be working for Gharst?"

She said with her face turned away from me, "Oh *prala* there is no denying I am not a chaste woman. I am bad, *m. alma* . . . no good for you," she whispered, peering up at me anxiously from under one arm. "But even an abandoned one has to eat and here I can eat better with less badness."

"You mean, Gharst—"

"That one cares nothing for women. For dinero only he makes covetous eyes. So long as my songs and my dancing bring patrons he cares not what I do in my room. In all Estados Unidos there is no one can dance," she said proudly, "like Soledad. Shall I show you, *prala?*" She reached round to unbutton the back of her dress, but I said:

"Later. This Gharst . . . what's he after? I mean, besides money?"

"I cannot tell you."

"He's friendly with Frunk?"

"He has much hatred for that one."

"What of the marshal, Bucks Younger?"

She shook her head.

"Red Irick?"

"He is a thing of this Frunk. Very quick with the pistol."

"How can I say? Sometimes he comes here. They do not speak to each other. I have not much understanding of this; only four weeks I have been here."

"And before?"

She shrugged. "Mexica, Queretaro, Zacatecas, Monterey, Laredo, Nueva Rosita, Juarez—my poor wandering feet must be always moving. Since I left the convent—"

"You received instruction? Then what of your people? where—"

"I do not know this. I think *los indios* . . . I recall

wagons, *soldados* . . .I have not the clear remembrance of this. The nuns of Panuco only. When perhaps I was eight I ran away with gypsies; it was too sad with the sisters. Too beautiful. Too still. They taught me to sing holy songs but the gypsies taught my feet to move."

She twisted round and sat up, caring nothing how much I saw of her legs. She had an expression of thinking. "Well, then, by myself I found how to fill my belly. A thing of the eyes, a little show of bare skin—men are such fools," she said contemptuously. "They think because of this I will share my bed with them."

She began suddenly to cry. Like a child. "I can tell what you think—a dancer! A frequenter of cantinas—an *orizica! Osté!* This is why you will not have desire of me—Oh, *querido mio,* you have tore up my heart and now—"

"Be still," I said, feeling strangely uncomfortable. "I have much gratitude—"

"Do I care about that? I speak of love and you—"

"Now wait—"

"*Por nada.* Keep your gratitude, gringo!" she cried, whirling up from the bed with her eyes like daggers.

ELEVEN

Two nights later I got out of there.

I was far from well but I was able to navigate and, soon as she'd left to amuse Gharst's customers, I climbed out of that bed and into my clothes. I had no plans, knowing well the futility of trying to lay out any given course of action when I didn't know what I was going to run into. I would

have to be guided by circumstance. The first thing of all
was to get out of this room.

I had to get hold of a gun. Since it was plenty obvious
I would run into trouble and equally certain I was in no
shape to put up any fight without weapons, my need of a gun
was paramount. I buckled the shell belt around my waist
and went over to the battered chest of drawers and went
through them.

Luck was with me. Among a bunch of junk in the bottom
drawer I found a pearl-handled 41-caliber derringer.
Loaded.

I tried the door expecting to find it locked but it wasn't.
In surprise and suspicion I stood with the cold knob gripped
in my hand and wondered if this were deliberate or care-
lessness.

It had been her custom to keep the door locked—"so that
no one, *mi alma,* will come in here and shoot you."

I stood crouched there listening while sweat came out
across the backs of my hands. This smelled like a trap and
the more I considered it the less I liked it.

Had she left it unlocked so that someone could cut my
throat while I slept or in the hope I'd get up and try to get
out? I could not believe the door was unlocked through over-
sight.

Speculation was useless.

If I left the room, and this were part of the plan, all the
breaks would be with the guy set to nail me. That was one
angle.

Then I thought of a better one. With this popgun in
hand I could get back in bed and, pretending to be asleep,
give whoever came in the surprise of their life.

But supposing no one came? I'd be a sucker for sure,
dawdling here wasting the best chance I might get. Luck
never liked a piker and it was tenet of the Rangers that
the man who took the initiative had the battle half won.

I opened the door and stepped out.

There was nobody on the balcony. The games down below were going full tilt. There was a fair sized bunch bellied

up to the bar. All the tables were filled and tobacco smoke hung in a haze round the lamps and the babble of voices was like the sound of cicadas. From a room two doors to the left of me I heard the low panting moan of a woman abruptly shut off by the scrape of fiddles as the platform buckaroos struck up a quadrille.

I took a quick look along that line of closed doors, wondering which was Gharst's. If I could get into his office. . . . There was a word in white paint on the third to the right, the one opening off the top of the stairs. It said PRIVATE.

Just as I got there the door swung inward.

"Ah—Trammell," Gharst said around his thin black cigar, and stepped away from the door.

I went in, kicked it shut and put my back against it. The light flashed back from his steel-rimmed cheaters. The bony mask of his face gave nothing away.

We stared at each other in silence.

Gharst cleared his throat. "I told you," he said in his dry precise way, "when you had anything to report you were to do it through Soledad. If you can't obey orders—"

"Never mind that. You wanted a Ranger. You've got one."

"Indeed. Where?"

"You're looking right at him."

"I'm in no mood for jokes," Gharst said dustily. "When I hire a man—"

"Rangers ain't for hire," I said, and tossed his roll of bills on the desk top. I saw the wriggle of the muscles along his jaw and pointed Soledad's derringer at his middle. "I want a gun," I told him—"one that'll shoot six times."

He eyed me a moment longer then went over and pulled open a drawer of his desk. My nerves went tight as catgut as he lifted out a long-barrelled Colt's .45. But he handed it over, butt foremost.

"My advice to you, Trammell, is to get out of this camp just as quick as you're able."

I said, "Unlock that back door—the one that goes down those outside steps."

He crossed the room, high and square and a little ungainly
in his high heeled boots, and turned the key without com
ment. But I could tell by his eyes he'd misjudged my inten
tions.

"Now open it," I said, "and start down the stairs."

His stare held a risen vigilance.

He stood there straight and motionless. "What do you
think that will gain you?"

"I'm not thinkin'," I said. "Turn down those stairs. And
don't make no quick moves. I'll be right behind you."

When we reached the street he swung about and faced
me. "Just what do you think you're about to do?"

"I'm going to get me a horse and I don't aim to lose
sight of you while I'm gettin' it. Strike out for the livery."

"There's horses across the street—"

"Head for the livery."

In the pattern of black and brightness induced by the
lamps of the roundabout dives his face showed the bony
mask of stubbornness. "To hell with you, Trammell. I've
gone far enough. You won't shoot me here—"

"There are smarter ways. Move out," I said, "if you want
to stay healthy."

It wasn't so late. There was plenty of traffic on the opposite walk and there were four or five riders coming up from
the turn into Canada Gulch. I couldn't afford to stand here
long and it was plain this was what Gharst was counting
on, that risk of exposure would force me to leave him.

"If I'm stopped," I said, "you're a gone goose, Gharst."

He didn't believe it but the habit of caution was too strong
for him to break. I could see the bitterness warping his
cheeks, the pale fury of hatred compressing his mouth
corners.

I flashed a look at the street.

Directly across from us, beyond the jammed walk, loomed
the cracked-plaster front of the Chinaman's hash house.
East of this, half obscured by a clutter of wagons and hitched
horses, was the bright facade of Frunk's Mercantile, its coal-
oil flares throwing dancing patterns of yellow radiance across

the black drift of the night's cruising shadows. Farther
down, perhaps two hundred yards from our placement,
where Canada Gulch spilled the rumble of ore wagons into
the town's main drag, was the dark huddled hulk of the
Eagle's rear end.

Our side of the street, by contrast, was practically deserted. A scattering of cowponies dozed at the hitch racks
before the dim front of Jack McCann's next door where,
sixty feet away, a group of high heeled shapes stood quietly
talking, silhouetted against the distant glare of the lantern-
lit porch of the Antler House, the last building this side of
the gulch's intersection.

I brought my look back and saw the tag end of Gharst's
glance coming away from that knot of dark figures before
McCann's. I watched him take the cigar from his mouth,
stare down at it a moment and then pitch it away. He fetched
out another and bit off the end.

"Don't light it," I said. "Shove it into your face and chew
it, and if those birds down the street open up as we pass
them, just toss their gab back and keep right on going. If you
stop it's liable to be the last stop you make." I moved
against him. "Get going."

With a frustrated growl Gharst swung into motion.

I dropped the gun in my holster and came abreast of
him on the side nearest the buildings, making sure in this way
he'd be between them and me when we reached the gabbers
lounged in front of McCann's. They might still make me
out, even with the barroom's lights in their eyes, but it was
the best I could do.

What I wanted, of course, was to get hold of my saddle
and dig out that five-pointed star of the Rangers I had
gone to such trouble to hide in its skirt. With that badge
pinned on me it might be tougher sledding to accomplish
my chore here but, at least, its significance might hold
back a few wild ones from cutting their wolves loose the
moment they lamped me.

There weren't more than ten or twelve gents in this camp
that would be like to know me if they got a good look.

Gharst and the marshal. Irick, of course, and Gideon Frunk
and the birds roosting round in his store when I'd been
there. It was this last bunch that bothered me for I couldn't
remember what a one of them looked like. Too much had
happened since then—and there was Short Creek. And the
one who had knifed me. And the ranny who'd sunk his blade
in Gharst's door.

Too many to keep tabs on and watch Gharst too.

I had to watch Gharst. From the moment we'd come face
to face in his doorway I had known he had made up his
mind about me. Give the guy half a chance and he would
bring this camp down on my neck like a twister. He didn't
want no Rangers snooping around. Right now every wheel
in his thinkbox was probably flying round like a kite in a
headwind trying to figure how to get me safely planted.

I tugged the brim of my hat down over my eyes and felt
my shoulder muscles tighten as we stepped onto the walk
that fronted McCann's and a couple of the gabbing group
twisted their mugs around.

"Careful," I muttered. "Take it easy now."

Gharst said nothing. His eyes turned narrow.

The riders who'd been coming up the street went past
and I saw the lone shape of a solitary walker round out of the
gulch and head this way on our side. Something about him
looked uncommon familiar. He came into the lights of the
Antler House and I recognized Bucks Younger, the marshal.

I choked back an oath. This could be the break I was
needing but it could just as easily work against me. Bucks
had sworn me in as a deputy, but that had been two long
weeks ago and I had no proof if he wanted to forget it.
Much may have happened while I'd been laid up. If he hailed
me by name all hell could bust loose if any of the gents in
this bunch standing around happened to be friends of Irick's.

I slanched a quick look at Gharst. He was watching the
bunch on the walk just ahead of us. One of the pair who had
turned around abruptly put out a hand. "Say—wait a sec,
Brian."

I could feel Gharst stiffen. His step faltered. I caught

hold of his arm. "Later," I growled, trying to hurry him on. But he shook me off. Stopped.

My eyes raked his face. He didn't know I existed—or that other guy, either. He was staring at Younger with an expression that lifted the hair on my neck.

Suddenly abandoning a lifetime of caution he let go with his voice in one high yell, made a grab at his side and whirled half around with his jaws wide open.

I stood stunned as the rest while he took three staggering steps and went down. Only, unlike them, I knew what the score was.

Black rage ripped through me. I'd been tricked like a fool.

I heard Younger running but all I could think of was how Gharst had outslicked me. Not content just to get me recognized, he'd made it seem like I'd killed him right in front of their eyes. And, by God, I was minded to do it!

Then I saw the blood leaking out through his fingers.

I DIDN'T hear the shot. It was probably drowned in the voice yelling *"Grab him!"*

That voice woke me up.

I jerked my gun out and ran.

My only chance was to get across the street and I bowled through that bunch like a ball banging tenpins. I heard Younger shout. I heard yells and cursing. Then the guns started barking.

I kept going. Doubled over, I made for the walk in front of Frunk's—reached it, and tore through that crowd like a bull through a mismanaged matador's cape.

I cut left, still running, still hearing that voice from the blackness yell *"Grab him!"* The voice was lost now but I remembered the sound and the vague swirl of shadows by the mouth of the alley that provided the boundary between the Eagle Hotel and Frunk's Mercantile. The same murky path I'd been up once before on the night I'd chased Short Creek away from Carolina.

It was Short Creek's face that I had in my mind, and

I'd have bet forty pesos it was him had dropped Gharst. By mistake, of course—he'd probably meant to drill me.

The passage mouth was barely ten yards away now. With heart pounding wildly and pain like a ragged blade between my shoulders, I redoubled my efforts. I aimed to nail that damned killer once and for all.

I barged into the alley and saw a running shape almost at the far end, blackly limned against the light from the hotel verandah. I didn't catch but a glimpse before he was out in the open with the light full upon him. I couldn't fire then—I was too surprised to squeeze trigger.

It wasn't Short Creek. It was Crafkin.

TWELVE

IT DID not take me long to reach the end of that alley but there was nothing to shoot at when I got there; Crafkin had vanished. The cottonwoods masking the bend of the river presented a wall of banked foliage as innocent of guile as a barefooted baby. Yet behind this surface deception, as I very well knew, lay a smuggler's maze of twisted trails down any one of which the man who didn't exist may have fled— or, with rifle butt cuddled to baleful cheek, even now be waiting a second chance.

Lit by its ten flaring coal-oil lanterns the deserted front of the Eagle Hotel looked for all the world like a painted stage set, the kind you could see at the Bird Cage in Tombstone. Set down in the midst of the night's deep blackness that brightly lighted verandah offered no chance of concealment.

I would have bet considerable Crafkin had crossed it and was inside even now, perhaps closeted with Carolina. I itched to make certain but was too well aware of the risk I'd be taking going up those bare steps. Too many bravos in this cutthroat camp would be glad of the chance to put a slug through me, and there was always the very real possibility that Crafkin had ducked into those riverbank trees.

Whether he had or not I couldn't stand here. Already I could hear the racket of pursuit avalanching into that murky passage.

I whirled to the left and trotted into the cottonwoods. The shadows beneath their boughs were like clabber, like a cloying fog that cut off all vision. What light came through their clustered leaves was deceitful, confusing, more a hindrance than help. I pressed deeper, stumbling on blindly till breath was a tearing rasp in my throat and slivers of pain thrust into my lungs from the half-healed hole the knife had left in my back. My foot snagged a root and I fell face first into cracking brush that filled my ears with a million echoes. Too spent to move I lay there, gasping.

A mutter of voices reached me dimly and boots drummed a hollow pounding from the planks of the hotel verandah. But I knew they wouldn't all go inside; some of those rannies would start beating the labyrinth under these trees.

I was right—too right.

I could hear them now, softly swearing in the shadows, the snap and crackle of brush as they drew steadily nearer.

I got to my feet, trying to still the sound of my labored breathing. I had the rank, pungent odor of mold in my nostrils and my face began to smart where I had scratched it with thorns. But all thought save flight left my head the next moment when, less than twenty yards away, I heard Irick's voice. "To hell with Bucks' orders! That bird's in here someplace—you think I'm a fool? He wouldn't cross that bright porch with all these trees growin' handy! Spread out an' quit jawin'."

They spread out and once more I heard the rustlings of their nearing progress. Alarmed as I was, I could still think sufficiently to realize if they heard me they would start throwing lead. I moved as silently as possible but, barely able to see where I was going and not being able to see at all what I was putting my feet into, I knew mighty well I was making enough noise for them to have no trouble placing me if they should all happen to stop together long enough to listen.

But I couldn't play possum. I had to keep going unless I wanted them to find me. It was a nerve racking business.

It presently crossed my mind to wonder what would happen when I eventually came to where there weren't any further trees and I had to move into the lonely open with Irick and his gun grabbers not more than a handful of yards behind.

It wasn't the kind of prospect to induce a man to tarry. I stepped up my stride as much as I dared. If I could put my hands on a tin can or bottle. . . . But if there were any such laying around in this thicket I would'nt be likely to see them or have any time for hunting. A plainly heard sound to their rear might turn Irick's gundogs, but I hadn't any means of producing such miracle.

As a matter of fact, I hadn't had much of anything since first coming into this camp but trouble, and it was bound to get worse before it got any better. I had long ago lost all sense of direction and might easily be going right around in a circle. Plenty of lost fools had done that.

Belatedly it crossed my mind if I could only be sure which way was the river—and could reach it—I might yet get away from Irick's pack. If I hadn't got turned plumb around in this tangle it had ought to be someplace off to my right, and on the chance it was, I headed that way. Almost anything, feeling the way I was now, looked better than being caught out in the treeless open.

I slogged along for awhile and then pulled up to listen. The sound of the hunters seemed to have become more distant, though I reckoned that was wishful thinking. I could still hear them plain enough, cursing as they beat their way through the bushes.

My head was spinning, every muscle throbbed. My nerves were pulled tight as fiddle strings. The pain in my back was a dull stabbing ache that was like the twist of a knife each time I drew breath.

Somewhere off to the left I heard the crash of a shot, then a drumming of others in swift succession—a confusion of shouts.

Some fool, I thought likely, had fired at a shadow. Ragged tempers would account for the rest of that racket. Now if only, I wished, they'd take off at some tangent . . .

They did. They came toward me.

While I paused, scarce breathing, to made sure of this fact, a dry stick snapped not twenty paces ahead of me.

I dropped a hand for my gun. Sweat cracked through the dry cold of my skin when the hand found the top of my holster empty. I couldn't believe it. But the big-barrelled gun Gharst had given me was gone. Gone, too, was the derringer.

Another stick snapped—closer. I heard the scuff of a boot. And then I couldn't hear anything but the nightmare crash of breaking brush as I fled through the night in headlong panic. More than once I fell, but scrambled instantly up, never pausing to take stock of the damage. I find it hard to believe I could have been such a fool, but I'll not offer excuses. I ran till I could not run any farther. The last time I fell I just lay there, retching.

When I began to take stock of my surroundings again the hunt appeared to be over. There was no sound in the brush. No calls, no curses. Never a bird disturbed the deep silence. It was a stillness like death, vast, impenetrable, undisturbed by even the chirk of a cricket.

I got to my feet feeling strangely light headed. I had no idea where I was except I seemed to be standing in some kind of trail. The dark bulk of massed foliage was over my head. On either hand the black tracery of straggling brush rose shoulder high without motion.

I was about to move forward when the uncanny depth of this silence assumed significance. It was too damned still to be natural, I thought. It had the quality of stealth, a stealth crouched and listening.

I tried to shrug the feeling away as absurd, as an aftermath of my crazy panic. But some instinct of caution would not let me move. I could only stand there feeling foolish—and then I heard it again. A vague rustling as though someone, very carefully, had moved aside a leafy branch.

Standing frozen in my tracks a moment later I heard the unmistakable sound of someone moving with the greatest of caution into the trail somewhere behind me.

I was frantic.

It took every vestige of will power I could muster to keep my feet from breaking into a run. Sweat stood out upon my cheeks like rain.

I tried to peer into the black labyrinth beyond. I looked over my shoulder, clamping my teeth shut to keep them from chattering. Nowhere could I untangle the real from the fantastic mirages night erected around me. I saw no one. Nothing moved, yet while I was twisting my face to the front again I caught the dry rattle of dusty leaves somewhere back in the brush that hemmed the trail's right hand. Out of the total quiet to the left someone grunted.

I pulled off my boots and once again stared into the pooled gloom ahead. I might step on a centipede or scorpion or put my foot on a rattlesnake, but dangers of this sort were vastly to be preferred to the volley of lead that would reward discovery.

With an extreme reluctance I crept forward.

I dared not stray from the trail lest I make some sound that would betray my location. Hardly daring to breathe I kept going, more frightened of those bravos closing in behind than of any risk of death I might face up ahead.

I came in time to a place where the path I followed was crossed by another. I hated the task of decision forced on me.

I had only three choices—left, right or straight ahead. I could not go back. I refused even to think of going into the brush. Already I thought to hear the pad of feet behind me.

Afraid to hesitate longer, I plunged left into the curdled gloom of the new trail but when next I paused, hoping against hope the ruse had been successful, the whisper of padding feet still came on.

It was uncanny, unnerving, to be tracked through the murk of this maze in such a fashion. My reason refused to believe anyone could do it, and suddenly I saw what must have been the true answer. There were enough of them after me that they could put a new man to every side trail likely to be encountered, and they were close enough to know if I went into the brush.

I pushed on, turning these thoughts over, trying to find some angle which might lead to a chance of safety or to some margin great enough to allow me to escape. Why, I wondered, were they content to remain behind me instead of closing for the kill? The only plausible answer I could think of was that they wanted me out in the open, that they were afraid in here they might shoot down some of their own crowd.

I began scanning the growth on both sides with more care. If I could find some place to lie doggo, some spot to hide out while they went hurrying past, I could then turn around and hit out on the back-trail with a pretty fair chance of getting away. But even as I considered this I knew it wouldn't work. They'd be watching for such a place as closely as I would.

I paused to listen again. Under my breath I cursed bitterly when I heard them still coming. They probably knew these trails. They certainly knew them better than I did. My best bet, I thought, would be to take a different turning every time a trail crossed mine; if I could do this often enough I might lose them. Say there'd been six of them after me to start with. If one had turned right at that last intersection and one gone straight on, there'd be not over four on my heels right now.

I concentrated all my faculties into trying to make certain how many were back there, but it was useless. For all I could tell there may have been twenty. If one had turned right and one left, and the other four had gone straight ahead on the main trail, there'd be just one behind me.

But I couldn't be sure. I couldn't be sure of anything—not even of how many had originally started. Getting up from the fall that had climaxed my run I'd heard three. If only these had followed me down that first trail it seemed a heap unlikely there was more than one still back of me.

It was at this point I realized I was standing in silence. The furtive footfalls had stopped. The pursuit, like myself, appeared to have paused to listen. I moved on. So did they. When I stopped again they stopped.

I gave up all thought of trying to conceal myself in the hope they'd go by. I went on, determined now to take the next fork right and put all the space that was possible between them and me without running. There was no chance, in my present shape, of outrunning them. I was finding it hard enough just to keep going.

Abruptly, without warning, I reached the end of the trees. Black open stretched before me in a vast fifty yards to the more intense black oblong of a tall unlighted building.

I gaped at it, stunned, plainly knowing I'd never reach it before pursuit broke cover. If I'd had any kind of weapon. . . . But I hadn't.

Then a second shock froze me. I recognized the building.

Sheer amaze locked all my thoughts while I stood eyeing it dully. It just did not seem credible after all I'd been through in that goddam brush; but there it stood in smug grim irony, as inscrutably enigmatic—as balefully dark and silent as ever I had found it.

I had come full circle. I was staring at my nemesis, the Eagle Hotel.

THIRTEEN

THOUGH I heard no sound behind me, I was not fooled into imagining I had lost them. Within easy gunshot at least one of Irick's crew was probably standing much as I was, scarce breathing, rigidly motionless, cocked to catch the ghostly tread of telltale footsteps.

A flick of the hand could prove or disprove this. All I needed to do was pitch my boots out into the undergrowth. Fortunately I had enough sense not to try it. The report of a gun would do me no good at all. The last thing I wanted right now was to attract attention.

I peered again toward the shadow shrouded front of the Eagle. Odd, I thought, how every trail led back to it. I had not realized this before but it was true enough.

This was the place Cap Murphey had sent me to. In its cramped and dingy lobby I had first met Crafkin and Short Creek. At its hitchrack I had smacked Bucks Younger, the marshal. In one of its upstairs rooms the body of the red-head's uncle had been found and in its lobby Irick had accused me of killing him. I'd been trying to reach its shelter when I'd stumbled over the corpse of fat Roy, and had again been setting out for it when loss of blood from that stab wound had dropped me off my horse.

Nor was this the whole score. In the alley separating its wall from Frunk's Mercantile I had rescued Carolina from a second installment of Short Creek's ardor and had, more recently, down its length chased the guy I thought responsible for what had happened to Gharst. Before its dark verandah I'd walked into Irick's gun and it was just over there that I had lost track of Crafkin.

Who was to say he was not inside *now?* And that iron-nerved redhead who had calmly told Younger's deputy no such fellow had ever been in her hotel! I'd long been hankering for a talk with her and it might just as well be now. If I could get there.

I took a look down my backtrail but discovered no more than I had seen before. A lot of black shadows. Any number of which could be concealing a man. Or several men.

If I waited long enough I thought it looked pretty likely that one of Irick's crowd might get careless enough or impatient enough to stir up some sound that would betray his location. But that wouldn't help me and in the meantime Crafkin, if he was still inside the Eagle, might take off for other parts.

I particularly wanted to get hold of that hombre for it was in my mind that this elusive cattle buyer might hold the key to many things. He was the only jasper I had ever caught sight of in proximity to Short Creek. They were both of them a heap too familiar with Carolina not to have any part in what was going on.

I had aimed to pack my badge to any talk I might have with Shellman Krole's niece, but that was out now. That badge was on my saddle which was probably at the livery or in Marshal Younger's office with God only knew how many crawlers and creepers between there and me.

Juning around at the edge of this thicket was only postponing the inevitable. Sooner or later they would jump me regardless. If I took to the open at least I might get a brief run for my money.

I stepped out of the trees.

The night was still as a strangled rabbit.

With a boot in each hand I moved toward the shrouded shape of the Eagle like I was walking on eggs.

Fifty yards doesn't sound like any great distance but it can be as far as hell and back. I advanced across that windless open with every nerve screwed taut as a drumhead and every muscle cringing from the shock of expected impact.

Nothing happened to disturb my progress. No shout ren

the night. No bullet touched me yet I lived and died a thousand deaths before the deep gloom of the verandah received me into its tattered obscurity.

Any instant I expected the alarm to go up, the dread hue and cry of the chase to begin. For aught I knew my approach had been noted by those within and perhaps even now was being prepared for. A step groaned in anguish beneath my weight but the die was cast. I could not turn back now.

Boots still in hand, my socks in shreds, I drove bruised feet across the cold planks of that silent verandah to bring up by the sagging screen of its door in a rash of chill sweat as my ears strained to catch any sound from beyond.

A dim mutter of voices came out of the quiet as water crawls out of a green-scummed seep. I could distinguish nothing but their low drone, their murmur—nothing whatever that would identify the speakers or even their number. The lobby looked black as a stack of shined stove lids.

There was nothing to be gained by remaining outside, nor did I wish to. From having used it before I knew the screen door would shriek like a stuck pig the moment I touched it, but the window was closed and might wail just as loud if I attempted to raise it. I took hold of the door and yanked it wide in one jerk.

It never let out so much as a whimper.

I closed it after me gently, not liking the thought that was in my mind. If the door had been oiled it had been oiled for a purpose and that purpose might not yet have been served. Irick could slip in just as soundless as I had, and all Irick's bravos, if I left it unguarded.

I got the chair by the desk and quietly laid it across the threshold and, with an equal stealth, slowly mounted the stairs with my feet squeezed as close to the wall as I could manage. I bypassed the third step which I remembered was warped but the eighth let out a most dismal groan.

I stopped with caught breath. My heart pounded, but the talk overhead went steadily on and, after a moment, so did I. I wondered what I would do if accosted. I might, I supposed, heave my boots at the fellow and perhaps after that put my head down and charge. Unarmed, it was about all I *could* do.

At the top of the stairs the sound of voices was plainer. There were only two—some man's and Carolina's. The man's had a gruff fed-up sound as though he were impatient with whatever the girl was saying.

This hall was not as dark as the stairs, its congregated shadows a little less opaque for the bar of light that came from beneath the left side's third door.

I was about to move forward when something blurred against the dim rectangle of the window at its end.

I might have dismissed it as pure imagination only something was there, less than twenty steps away, something dangerous and crouching. I was aware of its breathing, a suppressed winded sound that was almost like panting.

I became aware also that the window was open. I could feel the quiet draft from it curl round my ankles.

I drew back my right arm knowing a boot wasn't much but that it was better than nothing. Whatever was over there had come in through the window at about the same time I'd been coming up the stairs.

I was minded to edge nearer but stood where I was lest a floorboard reveal my presence and whereabouts. The unknown even now might have a gun trained upon me.

In the intolerable stillness I heard the girl say plainly, "But you knew all that—you knew we couldn't trust anyone. If you—"

The man's voice broke in, unintelligible but urgent, and Carolina told him, "If you can't do it I'll get someone who can! Or I'll shut the mine down. We're not operating Tailholt for the benefit of Frunk!"

The man said testily, "You've got Frunk on the brain. How could Frunk—"

Sharp through his words flared the rasp of a match. The draft whipped the flame out quick as it kindled, but not before I had seen what was facing me.

I let drive with the boot and flung myself after it. His goddam gun went off right in my face. Then I was into him, grappling him, slugging him, trying half blinded to get hold of the hand that was wrapped round his pistol. I got it, too, and smashed it into the wall—heard the gun hit the floor with a hell of a clatter. He slammed a knee in my groin and I reeled away from him, gasping, just as a door was torn open behind me. Lamplight, flaring into the shadows, revealed the tag-end of his drop through the window.

I caught the glint of his fallen gun and scooped it up, stumbling forward as his boots plucked wild sound from a shed roof. "Grab him!" I yelled, thrusting my head out the window.

It was too black to see him. I heard his boots strike the ground. Muzzle lights blossomed, rifles cracked viciously and, farther out, two more joined them. Someone ran through the shadows and Irick's bull roar spewed out balked fury. "Cut him down! Cut him down!"

Then a hand caught my shoulder, jerked me back from the window.

FOURTEEN

I FOUND myself staring at the biggest hunk of man I had ever clapped eyes on. Broad layers of flesh bulged the gray flannel shirt below the huge bald head and face of a shaved hog. He was like a stuffed pig but there was strength in him, too, and considerable consternation when he found the black bore of Short Creek's gun pointed at him.

He let go and backed off like he'd laid hold of a rattler. "My God! Who's this?" he wheezed, startled.

Then I saw Carolina. She looked plenty startled, too.

I guess I did look a sight with my clothes all torn from the brush and no boots on.

I saw her tongue cross her lips and she said, "Why did you come back?"

I motioned them toward the room. "Let's get out of this hall before that bunch chasing Short Creek find out they've been played for suckers. Pick up my boots, Fatty, and don't start nothing you ain't able to finish."

He didn't care much for that but he kept his mouth shut. He went and picked up the boots and shuffled back toward the door like the weight of the world was bowing him down. Carolina, with her eyes looking worried as well as frightened, said: "Now just a minute, Trammell. When I got you out of that jail—"

"Yes, indeed!" I said. "We'll go into that later. If those rannies come back before I get out of sight someone's liable to get their pipe dreams ruptured. I been pushed around enough in this camp. If there's any more shoving to be done I'll do it. Now get movin'."

I gestured with the gun. They went into the room, me following.

The fat man sagged into a chair that was too small for him and sat with hunched shoulders like he was figuring to be patient even though this didn't concern him. Carolina remained standing, cheeks flushed and chin lifted. I toed the door shut and put my shoulders against it.

They had a heavy wool blanket draped over the window and, to make sure doubly certain, they had the lamp turned down to where it wouldn't hardly have lighted up a half-grown junebug. "Pretty snug," I leered, "pretty cozy," and let my glance wander over to the bed.

The fat man scowled. Carolina's cheeks took fire and the look of her eyes would have made some guys uneasy.

But not me. Mad was the way I wanted her. "We're goin' to get right confidential," I said. "You want this sport to listen in on the powwow?"

"We have nothing to get confidential about—"

"Think again," I said. "And I ain't meaning that slick

little jailbreak you hatched as a means of getting me shot into doll rags."

"If you think—"

"Next time you figure to get a guy planted give your money to someone who'll go through with the business. Don't waste it on bunglers like Short Creek that ain't got hardly dried off behind the ears."

I gave her that and then I said before she could unfurl any back talk, "You went south a couple weeks ago an' chinned with Cap Murphey. You gave him a lot of guff about stuff goin' on at that mine your Dad left you, telling him you reckoned a gent named Frunk was tryin' his damndest to whipsaw you out of it, aided and abetted by the local law. You want to hear any more with this bird sittin' in on it?"

She was off her horse now all right. Her eyes looked like a couple of holes in a bed sheet. And a sour grin was twisting the fat man's mouth.

"I don't see how—"

"You will before I'm done with it."

Her head turned then and her glance met the fat man's. "You wantin' him to hear any more of this?" I said.

"He knows about that trip—"

"Does he know you been playin' drop the handkerchief with Short Creek?"

The fat man swore. "I told you—" he began, but she said angrily, defiantly:

"You told me not to go to Cap Murphey. You said getting a Ranger up here wouldn't do us any good—"

"Well, has it?"

"I had to do *something*. I couldn't just sit here and let them steal us blind. *You* couldn't stop it. Uncle Shelly wasn't getting anywhere. The bills were piling up and we hadn't anything to pay them with—"

"Making deals with crooks and killers—"

"I had to trust *some*body."

The fat man sniffed. "You certainly picked a lulu if you made any deal with Short Creek. You might just as well have gone straight to Gid Frunk. Hells bells! If you were going

to set a crook to catch a crook why didn't you hatch up
something with Gharst? At least—"

"I went to Gharst."

The fat man stared. "Maybe we do need a Ranger at that
Did you hire this gun-hung drifter too?"

"No," I said, "she didn't hire me."

"Then maybe we'd better save the rest of our linen to be
washed out after you've hit the breeze."

"It's a little late for that," I told him. "She should have
thought about that before she went to Cap Murphey—"

"What's he got to do with it?"

"If it comes to that, how do you stand in—"

"My name's Jeff Bender," the fat man growled. "I'm manager of the Tailholt Mining—"

"Yeah," I said, "you've done a whale of a job, you and
Miss Krole between you."

"By God," Bender said, "I don't have to take that!" He
started up from his chair.

I twirled Short Creek's gun by the trigger guard. "You'll
take anything I decide to hand you. Includin' the sack if I
reckon you need it."

His fists gripped the chair arms but he didn't get up.
"Who the hell asked *you* into this?"

"Your boss," I said. "I'm the Ranger she sent for."

He eyed me through a tightening silence.

The girl broke it up with an odd, nervous laugh. "You expect me to believe that?"

"You had better believe it if you want your mine saved."

"Let's have a look at your identification."

"I haven't got my badge on me."

She let go of a long breath and a deal of the nervousness
seemed to go out of her. A smile crossed her lips. "I thought
not. It was a good try, Trammell, but we are not complete
fools. You may as well put up your gun and get out of here."

I gave her a tough look. "Maybe this will convince you.
It was on a Friday you stopped off to chin with Cap Murphey. You arrived on the northbound stage from El Paso. As
you were crossin' the yard you happened to notice Joe Steb-

bins where he was painting the flagpole. You said, 'Hello, there. Is this the headquarters of Company D?" Joe allowed it was and kept right on paintin'—"

She looked startled. "How could you know that?"

"Because I was there—because I heard you. And I can tell you what Joe said—'

"Don't waste your breath," advised Bender. "You was probably there but that don't make you a Ranger. Only Rangers I've even run into packed stars—"

"I've got a star all right. But how the hell far would I get in this camp trottin' around with a badge on my shirtfront? You ever think about that? What I figured to do was poke around some before makin' myself known. I thought maybe that way I could get some kind of line—"

"You've got line enough, fellow. What you need is some proof."

"If that badge is what's sticking in your craw," I said hotly, "all you've got to do is to get hold of my saddle."

Bender grinned at me coldly. "*I* haven't got to get hold of anything."

I locked eyes with him. Carolina said worriedly, "What's your saddle got to do with it?"

"That's where my badge is, cached away in the linin'."

Bender looked skeptical. "Seeing's believing."

"Maybe you think I'm scared to go after it?"

He shrugged broad shoulders. "Not my worry." He stretched out his legs and crossed his arms behind his bald head. "If you want the plain truth, I doubt if you know what a Ranger's badge looks like. You come in here with a cock and bull tale—"

"No more cock an' bull than you've been shovin' about that mine!"

Bender jumped to his feet. I aimed the gun at his belly. "Take it easy," I said, "if you don't want to get hurt. If you're playing this on the level you've got nothing to lose by taking me down in that mine for a look."

"You're not getting near that mine until it's proved to my satisfaction—"

The girl said, "Just a minute, Jeff. I'm not inclined to believe him either but it will do no harm to look."

Bender threw out his hands. "All right. Go ahead." His eyes swept my face. A faint show of malice broke across his round cheeks. "Where's your saddle at?"

"If it's not at the livery then Bucks Younger's got it."

"What would Younger be doing with it?"

"When I got out of jail," I told Carolina, "first thing I did was make a run for my horse. Short Creek was waiting beside him with a gun out." I brushed in the highlights of my flight across the cliff, my subsequent return and desperate tussle with the knifeman, my sojourn at the Bellyful (saying only that I'd convalesced there and nothing at all about Soledad), my departure with Gharst and its sensational conclusion, my futile pursuit of Short Creek, my nightmare experience in the woods with Irick's gundogs and, finally, of how I'd run into Short Creek in the hall outside this room.

They heard me through without interruption, Bender giving me his winkless attention, Carolina's cheeks showing an increasing bewilderment fraught with anxiety that was almost consternation when I came to where Short Creek made his jump from the window.

When I finished she drew a long breath without speaking. She seemed paler than I could find reason for, in the grip of some inner turmoil that was far in excess of the emotion displayed when Red Irick had confronted us with the corpse of her uncle.

I couldn't tell whether she believed me or not but it was Bender's look that really gave me concern. His moon-round cheeks were inscrutable yet there was something in his manner that blew a cold wind of warning across my neck. There was some secret here, some dark stone being turned or cautiously lifted in the mind behind that unwinking stare.

I watched Carolina's tongue cross dry lips. "It's fantastic."

"A little unusual," Bender amended, "but not too out of line to be true. I particularly liked those references to Short Creek. If Gharst has been gunned I *agree* with Trammell that Short Creek undoubtedly is the one who did it—only, unlike Trammell, I think he did it deliberate. I'm not quite sold on the part, however, about Gharst in the role of Good Samaritan, patiently nursing our ailing Ranger—"

"He didn't know I was a Ranger until I told him so tonight. In fact, the first time I saw Gharst since I woke up in there was when I walked out of the place with him tonight. The only person I saw was Soledad."

"Did you find her very attractive?"

I looked at Carolina uncomfortably. "She was the one who took care of me—"

"Same thing," Bender grunted, still pursuing his thought. "She could hardly have gotten you up there without help, or even into the place without his knowledge. I think there's more to this than you've seen fit to mention."

"There's a little," I said, and told them about Gharst's remarks on conditions and his attempt to hire me to spy on Gid Frunk.

Carolina said nothing. Neither did Bender. He kept watching me with his reticent eyes and seemed still to be turning something over in his mind. "I suppose it has occurred to you that girl was Gharst's wife."

I must have looked pretty shocked. He grinned anyway and said, "You still haven't told us what Bucks Younger would be doing with your saddle."

"Before Miss Krole here got me out of that jail I had a visit from Younger. He was wise to what she was up to and said he aimed to let her go through with it if I'd agree to work as a kind of undercover deputy. . . . I suppose this sounds pretty loco to you. But Miss Krole had told Cap she thought Bucks was in on whatever Frunk was up to, and that she thought it was Frunk that was getting her concentrates. Playing deputy to Younger looked to me like a chance to find out if she was right—a better chance anyway than I was like to get otherwise. So I took him up." I met his glance and shrugged. "Couple days ago I asked what had happened to my horse and Soledad told me Bucks Younger had him."

Nothing further was said for several moments. In the glow

of the lamp Carolina's eyes looked as coldly disdainful as a pair of eyes could.

"So he made you a deputy," Bender breathed softly.

I dropped the gun in my holster, feeling uncomfortably like a fool.

"Well, it's all of a piece," Bender murmured. "Since Bucks obviously knows Carolina's dealt with Short Creek, I suppose he saw no reason why she wouldn't hire you. He probably figured you'd do better, and if he could get you into that mine—"

"All I tried to get Short Creek to do," flared Carolina, "was to keep some kind of watch on Frunk and see if he could find where our stuff was going to."

"And what did he find?" Bender asked, smiling thinly.

"Nothing, of course—I don't suppose he even tried. I was crazy," she said bitterly, "to ever think I could put any dependence in such a man; but I thought if the bribe were big enough—"

"What did you offer him?"

"The same thing I offered Brian Gharst. A quarter interest in the mine. The last time I met him he said it wasn't enough. He'd find out, he said, if . . . if. . . ."

Remembering the scene I'd come onto in the lobby and what little I'd observed in the alley that time, I hadn't much doubt about the terms he had offered.

Jeff Bender nodded and scooped up his hat. He clapped it on his bald head. He said, "We'll go take a look at that saddle now."

"Wait," she said. "He's no Ranger, Jeff—"

"We can quick enough find out."

"But there isn't any need to. I know you've plenty of reason to be disgusted with my meddling, but I'm not meddling now. I *know* this man's not a Ranger—"

Bender said thoughtfully, *"How* do you know?"

"Because I've already talked to the man Cap Murphey sent up here."

FIFTEEN

THE shock of her words struck clean down to my boot heels.

Through a magnified stillness Bender stared at her face and then his eyes came around and slammed into me roughly.

I had not realized this room was so large or that, heartbeat by heartbeat, it would continue to grow until it no longer had any walls at all. I had a queer sensation of standing alone at the top of a high place that was about to crash under me.

Bender's voice called me back.

I looked into their watching faces.

"He had nobody else to send."

Eyes blazing, she came a step nearer. "Are you calling me a liar?"

"No. You've been fooled. I'm not doubtin' you talked—"

"Just a minute," Bender growled. He said to the girl in a half strangled voice, "Is that the guy you sent down to the mine?"

She had no need to say anything. The defiance in her look was answer enough. Bender, swearing, shoved me toward the door.

But she got there first, put her back to it.

"Jeff—you've got to listen."

"Stand aside," Bender growled.

"You've got to!" she said fiercely. "You've got to give Joe a chance. After all, the mine's mine and—"

I got it then. I said: "Crafkin!"

Her eyes, wide and stirred, looked almost black in that light. She was like a young lioness in defense of her cubs, only it was love she was defending—or what she thought was love. Whoever this Crafkin was he'd taken her in completely.

Bender said, "Stand aside."

"No. You've got to hear me out. Joe's trying to help us and he will if you'll let him. He's been up against things like this before—in Quartsite, Superior, Globe and Goldfield. He's the man who broke up that gang at Bisbee. He's Captain Murphey's best—"

"Cap Murphey," I said, "never heard of that bird."

She ignored me. "You've got to give Joe a chance, Jeff! I'm not going to let you—"

"Now you listen to me, girl," Bender wheezed. "I've had all of your meddling I intend to put up with. When your father hired me to run that mine—"

"But the mine doesn't belong to my father any more," Carolina cut angrily into his words, "and I've lost all the money from this stealing I intend to. In spite of everything you've done we haven't taken one nickel out of that hole since Dad died. If I'm not to have any say in its—"

A loud crash and a curse from below chopped her words off.

We froze where we were, every one of us, listening. The corners of Bender's mouth pinched in. The girl's eyes looked enormous.

The hush got so thick it seemed like even the planks in the floor must be listening. I leaned nearer to Bender. "Irick and Company. I left the chair to the desk just inside the screen door."

Bender nodded. He said in a whisper, "We've got to get out of here. Douse the lamp, Carolina."

With infinite care and much grimacing I put my feet in my boots. I had had all the barefoot walking I wanted. I heard Bender take down the blanket from the window, heard him whisper to the girl, "Put it up after we leave and get that lamp lit again—"

"I'm going with you—"

I said, "Don't be a fool!" but, like before, she ignored me.

Bender got the window up while the girl made a knotted rope of bedsheets and blanket. Bender fixed an end of it to a leg of the iron bed and tossed the rest out the window. "Lock the door."

I took care of it.

One of the stairs creaked, and against the window's dim oblong I saw Bender stiffen. I guessed he was thinking what I was, that before we could ever all get to the ground they'd be into this room. It took no great amount of mental effort to picture them emptying their guns out that window.

Bender motioned us back. "Get under the bed."

We did. We got under it just in time.

Something hit the hall door with a hell of a thump. I heard the crack of its panel, another thump and the indescribable sound of splintering wood. Spurred boots made a racket across the floor. I caught the rasp of a match and beyond the bed's brace bar I saw three pairs of legs standing rigidly still.

Someone cursed. The match dimmed out. Boots rushed to the window and Irick's voice bellowed: "Crantz, Lefty— Barrigen! Wake up, you dimwits! They went out through this window!"

A fainter answering hail came up from the yard and Irick snarled, "You'll see something when I get down there!" and again boots hammered across the floor. When I heard them stampeding down the stairs I wriggled out from under the bed and got up. The girl got up too and Bender came out of the closet. "Let's have that lamp."

I handed it to him, saw him slip off the chimney and move to the window. Drawing back his arm he sent the bowl spiralling into the night and the glass chimney after it. We heard the bowl hit and then the crash of the chimney. Three guns began to beat up the echoes; and then Irick's bellow: "After them, you fools! They've ducked up that alley!"

I went over to the window and stood looking down into the cold pre-dawn shadows. I heard the in-an-out wheeze of Bender's breathing.

"Pretty cute," I said, "but that ain't going to keep 'em occupied long."

"Long enough," Bender grunted. "Come on. Let's get moving."

"Where?" I said.

"To the mine, of course." I saw his head twist around. Carolina's breath made a sharp indrawn sound. Bender's voice said imperturbably, "I want to see a couple faces when these Rangers get together."

Carolina said angrily, "This fellow's no Ranger! I told you—"

"You told me to give Joe Crafkin a chance. With considerable reluctance I've been giving him one. If I've been pampering a crook I aim to find it out pronto. One of 'em's lying and I'm going to find out which."

"You can prove Trammell's lying without taking him into the mine!"

"Very doubtful," Bender grunted. "He may have a badge in his saddle and still not be a Ranger. Also it's entirely possible he may be a Ranger even if that badge isn't where he says it is. I'll decide which is which when I get them face to face."

She wouldn't leave it there. She kept jawing about it after the way of all women.

At the foot of the stairs Bender said, fed up, "How the hell do you suppose I ran that mine before I had you to give me instructions?"

She shut up then and I said, "Where are we going to get horses?"

"We'll have to go on shanks' mare. It's not over three miles. I guess you can make it."

SIXTEEN

IT WAS plain Carolina wasn't liking this trip. Nor was she making any effort to conceal her displeasure, walking by herself like there wasn't another soul within a mile and forty rod of her. But I couldn't see how she had much to be riled over. If Crafkin, like she had made out to figure, was plumb on the level and a sure-enough star packer, she had everything to gain and not a particle to lose. Perhaps it had finally worked into her mind she might have made a mistake about that guy. If it had I guessed she would never admit it. She wasn't the kind that likes to be made look foolish.

I wasn't too crazy about this deal myself. I was anxious to get to the bottom of this business but I wasn't at all anxious to get myself killed. If this Crafkin was the kind of skunk I figured him to be, he was like to turn right ugly when the pasteboards hit the table. In my present condition, and after this damned hike, I wasn't at all certain I could shade him to the draw.

Neither him nor me would be much use dead.

From Bender's point of view it was an ideal situation and one that did him credit as a conniver of top strategy. He had nothing to lose one way or the other since he had made it plenty obvious he preferred to take care of the mine's troubles himself and without help or hindrance from anyone. The girl's accusations of incompetence meant nothing and, if he were honest, Bender's intention of facing us with each other offered a good possibility of ridding him of one if not both of us. And, if he were a crook, it offered the same advantages in addition to showing him which of us was the liar.

This dirt road through the woods to the west of the river ran fairly straight and almost due south and after a quarter hour of silent tramping I asked Bender where it was that Shellman Krole had disappeared. "Was it along this road?"

The mine superintendent nodded. "I suppose it must have been along here somwhere. So far as we can learn he never showed up in town; that is to say, before Deputy Irick came across his dead body. I think he may have been dead before he entered the hotel."

"What makes you think that?"

"The fact that no one's ever admitted seeing him. There's not many people that didn't know him by sight."

"How did he happen to be going to town?"

"He was going to pay a bill we owed at the store for groceries and mine supplies. He had thirty-five hundred dollars in his pockets when he said good-bye to me and took off. It was every bit of cash he could scrape up."

"Do you know if it was on him when Irick found his body?"

"If it was," Carolina said, "Irick got it."

"And the bill's not been paid?"

"Gideon Frunk says it hasn't. He's refused to give us any further credit—all part of his plan," she said bitterly, "to bring us to the point where we'll have to sell out to him."

Bender said after a moment, "It's a kind of vicious circle. We haven't milled any ore of our own for six months. The hotel's our last bet for getting further cash. All the concentrates we had on hand have been stolen. Through bribery and threats half our men quit and left us. Of those that remained there were so few we could trust I had to fire all of them but a handful. I thought I could manage to keep my eye on those but. . . ." He shrugged. "The stealing continues. Most of the ore disappears before I can get it to the mill. Whenever I do get a load or two through something happens at the mill and we have to close down. By the time we're ready to run again the damned ore's gone."

"What do you mean," I said, "about a vicious circle?"

"It takes cash to operate the kind of mine we've got. We're strapped for cash unless we can mill sufficient ore to produce the concentrates from which we normally acquire our cash. If we don't produce the ore we can't get the concentrates. If we don't get the concentrates to market we can't get enough cash to keep going. I don't say it's Frunk, though it may be. But somebody's carrying on a campaign that before many more days will shut the mine down."

"Suppose you tell me what's been happening."

Bender's fat made a shapeless shadow but I saw the upward jerk of his chin. "Everything's been happening. Every damned thing that could be calculated to stop us. As I've already told you, our crew's been reduced to where we're not getting out more than two carloads of ore to the day. The men won't work at night. We use tramcars to get the ore from stopes to shaft. From there it goes by hoist to the surface and, from there, in cars drawn by mules to the mill. We've had trouble with the hoist. Wheels have come off the tramcars. Mules have disappeared and other mules have been slaughtered. We've had cave-ins. We've had everything you can think of."

It was rough, all right. I began to see the magnitude of what Bender had been having to cope with. I didn't see any answer. But there had to be one because I had to solve it.

"When does all this stuff happen?"

"Any time. All the time." Bender's voice turned savage. "Up until lately most of the dirty work and all of the pilfering took place after hours. Then I put three men with shotguns in the mine with orders to shoot anyone they caught sight of between dark and dawn. They killed one fellow and that stopped most of the night work but—"

"How'd this guy get in?"

"We don't know. It's what's had me licked—how *any* of 'em get in. Up until just lately I've had eight men with rifles patroling our fence. It's a hog-tight fence that completely surrounds the property, including the mine entrance. The last couple weeks I've had three of those men inside the mine armed with shotguns—"

"Can you trust these fellows?"

Bender laughed shortly. "I play it safe as I can by rotating them, not telling in advance which trick they're going to

take. It's helped. It's cut the stealing down to a dribble—
and the damage. But it hasn't stopped either."

After a couple of hundred yards I said, "A thing big as this
ain't the work of no amateurs. Too much planning—there's a
pretty slick thinker back of what you're up against."

"I figured that much out two months ago."

"It's Frunk," the girl said. "He tried to buy the mine from
Dad. Dad wouldn't sell. Then, after they'd arranged that
'accident' that killed him, Frunk came to me and repeated
his offer. He upped the price two thousand, even finally
agreeing to cancel our bill at the store in addition."

"What was his best offer?"

"Twenty-three thousand five hundred—including the bill."

"I've heard it was closer to fifty thousand."

She laughed without mirth. "I can see you don't know
much about Frunk. What's been happening to the mine won't
cost a fourth of that amount by the time it's closed us down.
He has never been a man to throw away money."

"What do you figure the mine's worth?" I asked Bender.

"Impossible to tell. I haven't been able to get the vein
blocked out with any degree of certainty yet; I've been kept
too busy trying to keep in operation."

"Put a rough figure on it."

"I can't even do that."

"You can make a guess, can't you?"

"I don't see the point. It's obviously worth all the trouble
these fellows are going to or they wouldn't be doing it. This
isn't the work of ordinary *gambosinos;* it's a deliberate attempt to cripple the mine."

"Then whoever is back of it must be pretty well convinced . . ." I said, "Let's put it this way. Do you consider
it to be a more valuable—or potentially valuable—property
than Frunk's?"

"Signal Stope?" Bender shook his head. "I don't know
anything about the worth of Frunk's mine."

"You know what he's producing don't you?"

"No. He's working Chinese labor. We don't mill his ore.

He sends it to Douglas under a guard of twenty rifles. He's the only one who's able to send ore out of this camp."

"Well," I said, "what's happening to Tailholt is obviously the work of someone you're depending on to see that nothing happens."

"Some of the guards you mean?"

"Don't it look that way to you?"

"You'll have a hell of a time pinning it on any of them."

"You've got eight guards. You're keeping three of them in the mine. How do you go about deciding whose turn it is?"

Bender said scornfully, "I've thought of all that. I don't use any system. I pick three at random and they never know which ones it's going to be till I tell 'em to go on duty."

"Then they're all in on it and you'd better get rid of them."

"They probably are," Bender sighed, "but when you've saved a man's life it's pretty hard to suspect him of cutting your throat. I pulled two of those boys out of cave-ins. One of the others pulled me out of one. I try to keep one of those three in the mine with each shift. As for sacking the whole bunch, where am I going to get others that will be any better?"

It was knotty, all right. It was rugged as hell.

I saw lights up ahead. "That the mine?"

"Not that first batch—that's Signal Stope. The next ones are ours. They're at the mill. I keep 'em lit so our guards will have something to shoot by. We're not running the mill any more. And don't aim to until we get enough ore to be worth starting up for."

"What about Lucky Dog and Bell Clapper? Weren't they milling with you?"

"They were," Bender said. "I thought maybe if we shut down, one or the other of them might figure it would be worth their while to help us, but I reckon they're too scared of Frunk to risk it."

"What are they doing with their ore?"

"Sending it out with Frunk's wagons on percentage."

"It's getting through?"

"Why not? For half of their profit Frunk would help anybody. But us," he added bitterly.

I thought about that. I said, "How many men are you working?"

"Miners? Just three. And they're okay."

"Where was this guy Roy's mine—the fat guy that got killed?"

Bender pointed. I could see his arm against the near lights of Signal Stope. "Just this side of that first batch of flares. It wasn't a mine—just a hole in the ground. I imagine Frunk bought it just to get rid of Roy."

I studied the pattern of lights and judged the flares from the mill to be roughly five hundred yards from those of Signal Stope. I didn't hear any blasting. "Frunk's not working at night?"

"I don't imagine so. I heard he laid off the night shift some time ago."

"Right after my father was killed," the girl said.

It occurred to me to wonder if they'd run out of ore. But that didn't make sense. They would hardly be sending wagon trains to Douglas if Signal Stope's ore was in short supply.

I switched back to the killing of Shellman Krole. "We don't actually know that he was killed for money."

"Well," Bender grunted, "the bill *may* have been paid. Be a considerable job to prove Frunk's lying."

"Let me get this straight," I said, after a moment. "You've got a hog-tied fence around Tailholt's property which you're keeping patrolled by five men with rifles. Night and day?"

"They naturally have to sleep sometime. I've got eight guards in all. I keep three night and day inside the mine. One, night and day, patrols the fence."

"That makes four on duty all the time?"

Bender nodded.

"How many gates in that fence?"

"Just one. We keep it padlocked. One key's in my pocket. Carolina's got the other."

"It would be impossible, then, for anyone to get in or out without your permission? Without your personal attention?"

"Nothing's impossible," Bender snorted. "We've been losing both ore and concentrates. It's going out somewhere without my permission."

"Is the fence being cut?"

"It doesn't show any sign of it."

"Could the stuff be passed up over the fence?"

"I suppose it *could*. There's fifty-eight hundred feet of fence—one guard can't be everywhere or see every point of it every minute."

"Then maybe you'd be smarter to put all your guards on the fence—"

"I had 'em all on until the last couple weeks. We lost more before than we're losing now."

"You had more to lose. You were producing more, weren't you?"

Bender grunted.

"You've looked around in the mine? You don't think the stuff's being hid below, do you?"

"In the mine, you mean? No. I thought of that, too. I haven't found any sign of it."

We were abreast the lights of Signal Stope now. Two hundred yards up the slope there was plenty of activity where a huddle of weather-grayed buildings showed against the black bulk of the cliffside. A string of ore wagons were being loaded at the mouth of Frunk's tunnel and, off to one side, several men with rifles had their heads together, talking. No one bothered to look around as we went past.

"How close is that shaft to the mouth of Tailholt's?"

"Around a thousand yards," Bender said indifferently.

"How far are they down. Do you have any idea?"

"Around five hundred feet, according to rumor. They opened up that tunnel but, inside a little ways, they found they had to go down same as we did. They went faster, of course, using bigger crews—"

"How far down are you?"

"Two hundred foot level. Number 3 stope. Why?"

"Just wonderin'," I told him. But something was begin-

ning to click at last and the wheels of my mind were right
on the ragged edge of meshing.

"Well," Carolina said. "Here we are."

We followed her off the main road and onto a narrower
less-dusty one that led by gouged shelves to the eighty-
yards distant Tailholt fence. So far as I could see it was
pretty well lit by the tall flares that burned before the mill
buildings yonder near the end of the bench. Not a tree or
bush obscured the vision and just beyond the gate there was
a kind of sentry box overlooking the grounds from the relative advantage of a twenty-foot tower built of four-by-fours

Bender waved at the man in the cubbyhole, got out his
key and unfastened the padlock. After we'd filed through he
replaced the chain and snapped the big padlock shut again.
I followed them toward the black shape of the head frame.
I dropped back a bit and started off at an angle meant to
fetch me closer to the collar but Bender, twisting around
called me back. "We'll step into the mine office first, Mister
Trammell."

I followed them in.

A burly red-faced man with jet hair and gray eyebrows
took his feet off the desk and got up and came forward.
It was Crafkin, of course, looking much as he'd looked at
the Eagle Hotel. "How are you, Trammell?" he said, and put
out his hand.

SEVENTEEN

I watched his eyes and ignored it.

Carolina made a small noise under her breath. Crafkin
looking a little puzzled, finally took back his hand. He put

the hand in his pocket and jingled some coins. "How'd you like that bed?"

"Oh, Joe!" wailed Carolina. "Uncle Shellman was in it."

Crafkin's shape went completely still. In the lamp-lit silence I could almost hear the leap of his thoughts. A wickedness rolled across his cheeks. "Let me get this straight. You say your *uncle* was in it? You're talking about the bed I gave *Trammell?*"

She nodded. She told him of Irick's gruesome discovery, of how I'd been charged with her uncle's killing and of how she had gotten me out of the jail.

He looked at me oddly. "But why didn't you tell him you were here on Murphey's orders?"

"Where'd you get *that* notion?"

"What—"

"That I was here on Murphey's orders."

"Why, Cap told me—when he sent me up here to give you a hand." He considered me a moment. "You look surprised . . ." And then, "Oh, I see. You couldn't have known that, of course. I'd been over on the Blue tracking down a bunch of rustlers. Cap had written Mehrens he was awful short-handed and Mehrens sent me over. I got in just after you'd left." His eyes twinkled. "But why didn't you tell Irick you were a Ranger? Surely—"

"And tip off all the crooks in this camp? Krole wasn't killed. He was deliberately murdered. Bender here says he was packing thirty-five hundred dollars he was aiming to pay Frunk on their account at the store. Frunk denies getting it or seeing Krole, either."

Crafkin looked thoughtfully. "How do you know he was murdered?"

"He'd caught two slugs in the back and, near as I could tell, he hadn't been dead a half hour when I saw him. And there's a time lapse we've got to account for. According to Bender, he left here for town with that money on the morning of the 24th. On the 26th, still with no word of him, Miss Krole gets anxious and goes to Cap Murphey. It was late on the night of the 27th that Irick found him dead in that room at the Eagle. Where had he been in the meantime?"

Crafkin nodded. "And how did he get into that room?"

"Someone," I said, "got the jump on him. And not long after he left here. They may not have known he had that wad of jack on him, but it's a cinch he was either overpowered or knocked out and thereafter held prisoner until it suited someone's purpose to have him found dead in that room. He was put in that room to frame one of us."

"Or both." Crafkin nodded. "No doubt about that. But they couldn't have known about us when they grabbed him. I don't see yet how they could have known we were Rangers if you didn't tell—"

"I didn't tell anyone *I* was."

Carolina had kept silent as long as she could. "He doesn't believe *you're* a Ranger, Joe."

Once again Crafkin's eyes twinkled. "Well, you can't hardly blame him." He turned partway around and twisted up the bottom of the back of his vest. The yellow glow of the lamp gleamed back from the five-pointed shine of a silver star. He let the cloth drop. "This is Trammell's first detail. He knows he got the job because Cap had nobody else to give it to. Being merely on loan from Company C, and having pulled in after he'd already gone—"

"Let's get back to Krole," I said, feeling foolish. "How does—"

"I think you've figured it right. There's just one point. Krole was obviously overpowered, but I think that came later. Put yourself in his place. Packing all that money he'd be keeping his eyes peeled. I believe he reached town, or very nearly. I think he fell in with someone he trusted—or, at least, had no reason for particularly suspecting."

"He'd of been suspicious of anyone," Bender said. "Except maybe, Younger."

I stared, open mouthed. "But Carolina told Cap—"

"Carolina," Crafkin nodded, "suspected Younger of being hand in glove with Gideon Frunk. But Krole didn't. I've discovered that Krole and Younger were on pretty good terms. Krole believed Younger was trying to help him recover the lost concentrates. I think Krole met Younger that morning somewhere between here and town, told him what he proposed to do and asked the marshal to go along with him. They may have gone to Frunk's and paid the bill, some of Frunk's bunch—or Younger—overpowering Krole later."

He took a slow turn about the room. His saturnine eyes met mine, very thoughtful. "Frankly I'm not too fond of that notion. It's a deal more likely that Younger, on one pretext or another, persuaded Krole to meet him at, or go with him to, the marshal's office. I think he was kept prisoner there, or some place close, until Frunk got the happy inspiration of ridding himself of Ranger interference by framing you with Krole's killing."

"What makes you think it was *me*—"

"Several things. It's pretty obvious now that someway or other Frunk discovered that Carolina had gone to Cap Murphey. Granting that much, it becomes reasonable to suppose I was wrong in assuming they couldn't have known about us. They didn't know about *me* because I didn't sign the register and, at the time Krole was killed, I hadn't started to pry into things. I doubt if they even knew I was in town. They'd certainly no reason for thinking I was a Ranger.

"With you it was different. I think you were followed here by whoever it was they had tailing Carolina. The natural thing for him to do, once he'd learned her destination, was to hang around there until he learned what was brewing. When you left, he followed. I think, when you went into the Eagle, he reported to Frunk. Swift disposal of Krole became of paramount importance. Of almost equal importance, in their eyes, was the necessity of getting you out of the way before your connection with Murphey became public."

"But what if I'd come right out and said I was a Ranger—"

"To Irick? Irick's Frunk's man just as much as Bucks Younger. He'd have refused to believe you. You hadn't any badge. You had gone to see Frunk—perhaps the plan took shape then. He'd no way of guessing Cap had sent *two* Rangers; and you were already down in the book for that room. It must have seemed very providential to Frunk. By knocking off Krole and charging you with the killing he not only shut Krole's mouth but landed you right where a drink inflamed mob would have had no compunctions about stringing you up."

Carolina's breasts were stirred by the depths of her feelings and she turned to me, impulsively holding out her hand. "It looks as though I've had you all wrong, Trammell. You must think I'm—"

"I think you're mighty dang plucky," I said, taking her hand. "I owe you something for getting me out of that jail when you did. Not many girls would have had the courage—"

"The main thing right now," cut in Bender with some impatience, "is to get to the bottom of what's going on. Holdin' hands and chin waggin' ain't going to put any ore in the crusher."

A more lively color touched the girl's cheeks. She took back her hand and Crafkin, looking at Bender, said, "Have you posted Trammell on what's been happening?"

"I've told him about it," Bender grunted. "Only thing I ain't mentioned is the stolen timbering that disappeared out of the south end of No. 14. Carrie," he added, showing the edge of a sour grin, "ain't been too happy with the way I've been handling this business. Now let's see what you two sleuths can do. This ought to be duck soup for a pair of smart Rangers."

"We'll sure do the best we can," Crafkin smiled.

Bender's allusion to Carolina's dissatisfaction reminded me of that fragment of talk I'd overheard at the hotel. *"If you can't do it,"* she'd said, *"I'll get someone who can! Or I'll shut the mine down!"* She'd been dissatisfied all right or she never would have tried to do business with Short Creek. Or with Gharst.

What I hadn't been able to understand was why, if she was dissatisfied, she had not fired Bender. A misplaced sense of loyalty might, of course, have accounted for it; or she may have been afraid she couldn't replace him, or been afraid the replacement could have done no better.

These were thoughts which had crossed my mind. But now another thought came and I said to Bender, "How much longer does your contract run?"

"If it's any of your business it runs another three years."

So that was that. But I didn't leave it there. I said to Carolina, "Was it just his handling of this thing that bothered you?"

Her glance was puzzled, "I'm not sure I understand."

"I mean you hadn't any reason to suspect he wasn't trying? You trusted him, didn't you?"

Her startled face was very lovely. "But of course. I still do. Jeff was one of Dad's closest friends—it was why he hired him."

"Did he share your father's belief in the mine?"

"I'll answer that one myself," Bender growled. "Sam Krole thought he had the world by the tail. He thought he'd found another Comstock. There seems to be plenty of ore but it has to be mined. You don't pick it up like candy off a counter."

"How big a bunch do you reckon we're up against?"

Bender shrugged. "Not too many, I'd say. For most of what's happened two or three could have done it."

I slanched a glance at Crafkin. "You're wrong about Younger. I don't think he had any part in Krole's death."

Crafkin said skeptically, "Who else could have taken him in like that? Certainly not Gharst. Not Frunk himself, nor Irick. Who else does that leave you? Packing all that money, you know mighty well he'd have been watching for trouble—"

"He could have been waylaid."

"He could have been, sure. But why don't you want to believe it was Younger?"

"He just don't strike me as that kind of a gent."

"Well, it don't make much difference who trapped Krole. You can't get around the fact he was killed, or that the killer did his best to tie the job onto you."

"I'll take that," I said, "and I'll accept it as highly probable that Gideon Frunk is after this mine. Bender says
there have been quite a number of cave-ins, that timbering's been stolen and, I suppose, tunnels blocked." I looked
at the mine boss.

Bender nodded.

"But none of these things have actually ruined the mine.
It would have been just as easy, wouldn't it, for them to
have hidden a stick of dynamite in the ore being sent to the
crusher?"

"Of course," Bender said. "But—"

"So it's plain as ploughed ground that whoever's behind
this has no intention of really ruining Tailholt. That's why
I'm willing to believe it might be Frunk. But it doesn't have
to be. It could just as well have been Gharst."

Carolina said, "I don't think it was Gharst. I'm pretty sure
it wasn't. He wasn't a bit interested in my proposition. He
said that Bellyful Bar was all the mine he had time for."
She shook her head. "It's Frunk. I *know* it's Frunk. Right
from the very beginning—"

I said, "It could be Bender."

Bender's look showed a startled anger. He came half
around with his big fists clenched and a baleful scowl on his
shaved hog features. Then his great shoulders loosened.
"This ain't no time for jokin'—"

"I'm not joking. Nor am I accusing you or anybody else.
I'm just pointing out a few possibilities. It could be Bucks
Younger, as far as that goes. Whoever it is, he obviously
believes this mine is worth all it takes to get it. When a
man doesn't stop at murder he's not going to balk at anything else."

After a moment Crafkin nodded. "I'll subscribe to that.
Have you any idea how we're going to stop him?"

"I've got two or three notions, though I doubt if you'll
like them."

"What I like or don't like is hardly important. You're in
charge of this case. What do you have in mind?"

"For one thing, I'd like to get Bucks Younger down here—"

Bender jerked up his head. "Over my dead body!"

Carolina was plainly against it. "What good will that do?"

"I don't know," I said, "but I'd like to find out."

Crafkin, eyeing me keenly, said, "You want Frunk, too?"

"I don't think we'll need to ask Frunk," I said. "Just let me have Younger here for six or eight hours and I believe I'll get to the bottom of this business."

I saw Carolina toss a quick look at Crafkin.

Bender scowled. "That's a damnfool notion. Where is the sense of hiring all these guards if—"

"There's no sense in hiring them. You've already proved that." I said, "They're as worthless to this mine as that fence you've put up. You're still havin' trouble and you're still losing ore."

Crafkin said, "What do you think, Carolina?"

She drew a long breath. "I don't know. I've never trusted him. I can't really put my finger on it but there's something about the man. . . ."

"You think he's two-faced?"

She considered that a moment, lifted her shoulders and let them fall. "I don't actually know one thing against him. Uncle Shellman *did* trust him; he believed Bucks Younger was doing all that he could. . . . But just the thought of the man—I don't like him."

"Then you'd rather not take the gamble?"

"Let me ask you one thing," she said quietly. "Why do you feel that Younger's presence would help you?"

"Let's call it a hunch. I think your uncle was smarter than he's being given credit for."

Her face showed surprise. Her eyes revealed interest. "How do you mean?"

Even Bender leaned forward.

"I think," I said, "he'd got hold of the answer. Or he was gettin' damn warm."

I could feel their thoughts taking hold of this. In the lamp-lit silence Crafkin's eyes looked reflective. Bender's beefy cheeks were still.

Carolina searched my face. "You really believe that?"

I said, "Consider the fact. Your uncle got his living from the Eagle Hotel."

"Yes, that's true," she admitted. "He hadn't any share in the Tailholt properties. By the terms of Dad's will he was named executor and made my guardian. The trouble at the mine upset him."

I said, "Naturally. He was responsible for seeing that the mine showed a profit. He must have realized someone was attempting to cripple it—"

"He believed it was Frunk. The same as I do," she said.

I merely nodded. "He wasn't the kind to shirk his responsibilities. He was trying to find out what was going on and stop it. If he thought Younger could help him he must have had some reason. I think you've been confusing Irick's actions with Younger's. I don't believe Younger is Frunk's man and I've a hunch if we get him down here he will prove it."

"That may all be true enough," Crafkin said. "But the thing we're interested in proving, it seems to me, may not have anything at all to do with Bucks Younger."

"We were sent here," I reminded him, "to locate Shellman Krole, to find out what was happening in this mine and to stop it. If Krole believed Younger could help him get to the bottom of it there's no reason to believe Younger couldn't help us."

Carolina, still watching my face, said, "Then let's try it."

"We don't know," Bender pointed out, "that Shellman actually thought Bucks Younger could help him."

"We know *you* weren't able to give him much help."

Bender's shaved hog face looked at me without expression. "All right," he said, "go ahead and fetch him down here." He stared a moment longer. "Rangers!" he snorted, and rammed his hands in his pockets.

He was halfway to the door when Crafkin spoke. "What are you figuring to do when he gets here?"

"Search the mine," I said, and saw Bender stop.

He took another long look at me over his shoulder. "And what the hell good do you think that will do?"

"I've a hunch it may show us what they've been after."

EIGHTEEN

"AFTER?" Carolina's stare swept from me to Bender. She drew in her breath with an increasing bewilderment. "Am I being awfully dense?"

The mine boss' beefy shape swung round and he wheezingly came a few steps back with his rolled-up sleeves looking baleful as the hackles of an angry dog. "I thought it was your notion they were after this mine?"

"It was."

"Then what in hell are you tryin' to pull now?"

"I'm trying to find an answer that will fit all the facts."

"What facts?" asked Crafkin, pressing the lips of his leather-dry mouth together.

"Some of the mismated facts that right now don't gee."

"Like for instance?"

"Like why would anyone take such risks for a mine you claim ain't no better than good?"

Bender leaned forward. "How many mines have you bossed in your time?"

"I haven't bossed any."

"You've worked in a lot though?"

"Nope."

"You're an authority on ore?"

"Not an authority—"

"Yet you've got the gall to come rampagin' in here and

make it appear I'm either a crook or don't know my business!"

His shape began to swell like a toad. I could see black rage rousing back of his stare but I shook my head. "You don't have to put words in my mouth. If I thought you were a crook—"

"Then maybe you think I don't know my business?"

"I don't believe he means that," Carolina soothed. "I think probably, Jeff, he means we may have overlooked something—some kind of thing an outsider might notice." Her glance sought my face. "Isn't that what you were thinking?"

I wasn't paying much attention. Something Bender'd said had set a train of thought to rolling and an entirely new concept of unglimpsed possibilities was opening before me.

"Isn't that what you meant? Jim!"

I stared. I said absently. "Maybe it *is* Frunk. Maybe he's back of this whole crazy business. But if Bender has figured the worth of this mine right. . . ."

"Oh, he has—I'm sure he has," urged Carolina.

I met Bender's black stare. I said, "Joe, go fetch Younger."

Bender pulled up his chin. "I guess you know what you're doing. I guess you know Younger and Short Creek are brothers."

I hadn't known that but I wasn't much surprised. Quite a few of the pieces were dropping into place. "The best of families have their black sheep," I said. "Go ahead, Joe. Go get him."

Crafkin looked at me carefully. He took in a long breath. He started to say something, changed his mind, and still looking reluctant, finally moved toward the door.

"And fetch my saddle," I called after him.

"You've played hell with things now," Bender snorted. Then he shrugged. "There'll be java on the back of the stove in the cook shack. I suppose, if you're hungry, I could fry up some beans—if you don't mind trustin' my hand with the skillet."

"I guess I'd trust you that far." Through the window I

could see it was getting light fast. "What time will your crew be going into the mine?"

"They don't work on Sundays."

It kind of surprised me to realize it was Sunday. Where had the time gone? There was concern on Carolina's cheeks. She touched my arm timidly. "You ought to get some rest," she said. "You look like you've been through the crusher."

"I'll make out. What about the shotgun shift?" I asked Bender.

He consulted his watch. "They'll be up in five minutes. I better go wake the others—"

"Let them sleep," I said. "We're going to pull the guard off."

"Pull it off?" His jaw sagged. Then he clamped his teeth. "That the way you want it?" he asked Carolina.

She looked at me uncertainly. "Do you really think we should?"

"If you're satisfied," I said, "why did you go to Cap Murphey?"

She chewed her lip in silence.

"Look," I said, too weary to argue. "This stealing's been going on a good while now. Your uncle tried to stop it and got killed for his trouble. You've given Bender a chance. You've tried your own hand at it. The mine ain't made a nickel in months. If you want this stuff stopped—"

"Of course I want it stopped." Her voice had an edge to it. "Do you think I enjoy—"

"Then put me in charge."

"But what if you're wrong?"

"Hell's fire!" I snarled. "Can I be any more wrong than you? Or Bender?"

Her cheeks turned white, then red, then white again. "What do you propose to do?"

"Get rid of these rifles. Disarm the whole bunch and put them outside the fence."

Bender's eyes altered. "The shotgun guard, too?"

"The whole damn works!"

Bender shook his bald head. "I'll go put on the beans—"

"You'll stay right where you're at until we get this thing settled."

His look wasn't any more rabid than mine.

Carolina said, "Well . . ."

I said: "Make up your mind."

She didn't like it. But she gave in a lot sooner than I'd expected her to."

"All right," I told Bender, "we'll go over to the collar now—"

"The mine guard's come up. They're over in the change house—"

"What have they done with their shotguns?"

"Probably left them in the cage," Bender said. "That's what they usually do."

"Call that fellow down out of the monkey box."

Bender stepped to the door. When he came back I said, "What'll those birds in the change house do now?"

"Soon's they get dry clothes on they'll come over here to find out when they're on again."

"How do you get hold of the four that're sleepin'?"

"They'll be over."

I heard footsteps outside and a mumble of talk sound. The man from the tower came in with three others. I said, "You fellows just stand around for a minute."

Pretty soon the other four came in. "Give Miss Krole the key to that padlock, Bender."

Bender grinned sourly and gave her the key.

"All right, boys," I said. "You're going to have a day off. Miss Krole's going to let you out the gate. This treat's on the mine; you'll be paid same as usual. Be back at the gate at six sharp in the morning."

Several of them turned curious faces toward Bender but he kept his mouth shut and they followed her out. Bender went over and stood by the window. "You can go fix them beans now," I told him.

When Carolina came back she looked worried. "Where's Jeff?"

"He's gone to warm up some grub," I said. "He won't run away."

That fetched her head around sharply. "You don't like him much, do you?" She looked tired and discouraged.

"I suppose you locked the gate up again?"

"Wasn't I supposed to?"

"I don't guess it much matters. You can give the key back to Bender."

"Aren't you afraid he might decide to let the men in again?"

I looked at her then. But I didn't say anything. I went over to the window and peered up the road. The sun's welcome smile was gilding the ridgetops but I couldn't see much. Brush grew too thick between the Signal Stope and town and the twisted excuse that passed for a road was too fogged with dust where it dipped through the hollows. "How long," I asked finally, "do you reckon it will take them?"

Carolina shrugged. "He had his horse. Not long, I shouldn't think, if he was able to find Younger. Are you satisfied now?"

"About what?"

"About Joe."

"Crafkin?" This was dangerous ground with her feeling about him the way she did. "Satisfied how?"

"About him being a Ranger?"

I wished like hell she hadn't asked that. But she was going to have to know the truth sooner or later. I remembered the blood leaking out through Gharst's fingers and the running shape scuttling through the gloom of that alley.

"Joe Crafkin," I said, "is working for Frunk. At least . . ."

Her eyes were coldly despising me.

I let her have it then without wrappings or ribbons. "He's no more a Ranger than Cap Murphey's pig!"

Her voice tore into me. "You saw his badge, Trammell!"

"You're damn right I saw it—*and the mark I scratched on it!* That guy's been lying from the minute you laid eyes on him. Even that fight in the lobby was faked—d'you think a bravo like Short Creek would of taken that pounding without he was paid to?

"Get your eyes open! It was Crafkin followed you down to Cap Murphey's; it had to be him for Frunk to know about *me*. And then he gave me his room with your uncle dead in it and, when that didn't stop me, last night he tried again and dropped Gharst by mistake."

She stood without breathing with her eyes gone as black as holes burned in a blanket. Her voice was a whisper. "I don't believe it."

But her look told me different.

I drove a couple more nails in. "After Gharst went down I chased the killer up that alley. I've already told you I thought it was Short Creek; but when that lantern light hit him I saw his face plain. And now we come to the badge you been settin' so much store by; Short Creek stole it. After I'd signed the book I went back outside to fetch in my bed-roll. Short Creek was out there going through my belongngs. Joe didn't steal my badge. But he's *wearing* it."

She was convinced. No doubt about that. I could have felt damn sorry for myself about then.

I said, "Don't look so damn sick. I've been a fool, too. Come on." I took her arm. "Bender's callin' us."

She jerked away from me, shivering. I didn't much blame her. In her place I would have hated the sight of me.

"What are you going to do about . . . him?"

"Nothing, right now. I'm going to give him some more rope."

"Hoping he'll tangle up someone else in it?"

She looked pretty bitter. "That could be a big help," I said.

"Why did you want Bucks Younger?"

"Your uncle trusted him. Besides," I said "I'm probably going to need some help. These fellows ain't playin' for marbles, you know."

She tried to pull herself together.

"You better come and put some hot grub under your belt."

She shuddered. "I couldn't."

She came after me though. Maybe she just didn't want to be left alone. You never can tell about a woman. I wondered if she was figuring to tip Crafkin off.

She turned to me again as we stepped into the cook shack. "You will admit, won't you, that I've been right about Frunk?"

"About him tryin' to grab the mine? Sure. He's doin' his best. He's the one that's got your ore, all right. Probably been back of most of your trouble. But he ain't the only one."

Bender, busily eating his breakfast, stopped with a forkful of egg in the air. Then he shoveled it into his face and kept chewing. It was Carolina who turned clear around and said sharply, "Ain't the only one! You mean someone else is after it, *too?*"

I said, "From where I stand that's the way it ravels out. Why else would Frunk try to put Crafkin in here? Not to speed up his stealin'—he's getting it now fast as Bender can mine it."

The mine boss scowled.

I scooped two fried eggs and some beans on a plate. "You better have something," I told Carolina.

She shook her head, sagged into a chair. I took the plate to the table with a cup of black java. It was the first chance at grubpile I'd had in some while and I went right to work on it.

After a couple of minutes Bender shoved back his chair. He twisted a smoke and said as he licked it, "About that crack you just made. Who do you think in this camp is big enough to fight Frunk? Besides Gharst, I mean."

"Gharst wasn't after this mine. Like he told Carolina, when she went to him for help, he had all he could take care of."

I took a big gulp of coffee, swashed it round through my teeth. "There's two separate parties trying to get Tailholt—Frunk and some other bird. Frunk set the ball rolling. This other guy, then, caught the drift and bought into it."

"How do you arrive at that notion?"

"Considering the state of Tailholt's resources—which are practically non-existent—do you think any fellow with the influence, manpower and cash Frunk commands would take this long to put a mine out of business if there wasn't someone else cuttin' in on his program?"

Bender lit his smoke.

"Consider the facts," I suggested. "Krole, the mine's founder and original owner, was made a proposition by Frunk which he turned down. Shortly thereafter, about six months ago, Krole gets killed in some kind of 'accident'. Again Frunk offers to buy the mine, this time from Carolina. But her uncle advises her to hang onto the property and starts digging to find out why Frunk wants it. All sorts of things get to happening. You lose mules and tramcars. In addition to the thieving which was already going on, you start having cave-ins. Tunnels get blocked. Your miners get trapped and bought off and scared off. Finally, in self-defense you have to let most of the rest go. Then uncle disappears. Carolina goes to Murphey for help and somebody follows her. Krole, two days later, turns up dead in his own hotel, killed in such a manner as to implicate *me*. These things I believe, or the most of them, can be charged against Frunk. He may have killed Krole or had him killed, but he didn't waylay him.

"I knew he'd been tied when I saw the way his shirt sleeves were wrinkled. For two days somebody had been holding him prisoner. But not Frunk. And it wasn't Joe Crafkin because Joe is Frunk's man just as much as Red Irick is."

Bender's eyes widened. "You mean Crafkin's not a Ranger?"

"Did you ever think he was?" I told him the things I'd told Carolina. "But those aren't all the reasons I had. Why hadn't he told Carolina about me? Why did he insist on giving me his key before he'd even got out of the room? Why wasn't his name on the book? Obviously because he was busy laying pipe that would give Red Irick an apparent basis for charging me with Krole's killing. This tie-up with Irick proves Joe is Frunk's man."

"But if Frunk's crowd didn't engineer Krole's disappearance," Bender said, "how did his body get into that room?"

"I think Frunk discovered what had become of him. I think one of his men, when the time was ripe, staged a fake rescue and, after selling him the notion he was in friendly hands, talked Krole into going to the Eagle. Not much risk of anyone seeing them. No moon that night. Carolina wasn't there; she'd gone off to meet Short Creek. They'd already put the verandah lights out. Frunk's agent, probably Crafkin, took Krole into that room and shot him."

Bender sighed, looking immeasurably older. "It had a sound, all right. What about this other bird— the feller you say is bucking Frunk?"

"He'll be around."

Bender lifted his head to scowl at me. "Is that why you sent all the guards off to town?"

"It's why I told them to report back tomorrow. Seemed a good idea to let him know the field was open. That news will get around. Shouldn't take him very long to come up with ten if we give him four and he has six already."

"What in the world—?" Carolina stopped.

Bender's lifted glance showed a jerky brightness. "You want him to guess we're searching the mine?"

I grinned at the sweat cracking through his skin. Carolina said tightly, "You mean to use us for *bait?*"

"Not you. You're stayin' out of this."

Our eyes met and locked. Her cheeks were pale but her tone was like granite. "If you're going below I'm going down with you."

Bender scowled. "Do we have to take Crafkin and Younger? If you're right about—"

"We can keep our eyes on him."

Bender said irritably. "We haven't got eyes in the backs of our heads." He ground out his smoke and got up, still frowning. "If this other bird hears we've pulled all the guards off you can bet your bottom dollar Frunk will hear about it, too. You thought about that?"

"I'm countin' on it."

Bender stared, and suddenly swore. "You're loco!" He flung a look at Carolina. "It's too risky, I tell you!"

I asked if he knew any better way.

He was right about the risk, of course. It would be damned risky. Already the word would have spread through the camp. *No one at Tailholt but the owner, her mine boss and that gun-hung drifter that broke out of jail.* That would bring them, all right. They couldn't pass up that.

"You want to flush 'em out where your law can get at them, and maybe you'll do it," Bender said grudgingly. "But why go into the mine to do it? Why not just—"

"They'll be watching for tricks. We have to make this look good. We're supposed to be trying to find out what the score is. If we don't go into the mine they won't show—"

"And, if we do," Bender said, "they may damn well try to bring the whole hill down on us. You're offering them the chance and that's all that will fetch them."

"But first," I grinned, "they'll make sure we're down in there. And that's when we'll grab them. They'll have to come down. Neither one of those birds will ever be satisfied unless he can trap the other guy with us."

"What about the marshal and Crafkin? If you're right about Crafkin—"

"That's why I want Younger in on this. He's no fool. He knows about Joe and that room at the Eagle."

Carolina said tightly, "Does he think Joe killed Gharst and my uncle?"

"I don't know but—" I stopped. I looked at her, careful. "How did Joe get through the fence with that gate locked?"

Carolina flushed. "He had my key—"

"How *long* has he had it?" That was Bender talking and he did not look pleased.

"I gave it to him when I sent him over here to see you."

Bender glared at me, exasperated. "You see how it's been? *I* didn't know he had a key to that gate." He said, looking madder, "I never know anything till after it's done with!"

"When'd you send him over?" I asked Carolina.

"Four nights ago—"

"And he never showed up until the day before yesterday!" Bender swore. Then to me he said, "Will he fit the picture you have of this 'other guy'?"

I turned it over, finally nodding. "He *could* be the guy. He's been working for Frunk. If he's managed to discover why Frunk's after Tailholt, I wouldn't put it past him to try and grab it for himself. He's—"

Bender, stopped before the window, said: "They're out there now. Him and Younger are at the gate."

NINETEEN

HE STEPPED into the yard.

"I can't trust that fellow," Carolina complained. "There's—"

"Bender?"

"Bucks Younger. If you had seen him and Frunk hobnobbing round before you—"

She was hipped on the subject. "How come you put so much trust in his brother?"

"Short Creek? I didn't."

"You tried to use him—"

"I tried everything. But I didn't trust any of them. Except Crafkin." The bitterness of remembrance chased color through her cheeks.

"Smooth customer," I nodded. "He's puttin' on the charm act out there now. When did you first come across your uncle's body?"

"When I was taking fre—" She caught her breath on a gasp, her staring eyes grown enormous. "How did you—"

"When we went up there with Irick you had so much on your mind you forgot to show shock. It gave me the notion you might have killed him yourself, or had him killed. While I was flat on my back over at Gharst's I realized you must have known he was up there. That put sense in a lot of other things that had me fightin' my hat; your insistence on me writing my name in the book, your denyin' there was any such fellow as Crafkin. You were doing everything you could to cover him."

"I couldn't believe he was guilty. I thought Frunk was framing him. Even after I felt sure he must have known uncle was up there I couldn't bring myself to. . . . But when he came back the other night he said Shellman hadn't been there when he gave up the room. Even then I wouldn't let myself really become suspicious. I was sure that wasn't true but—"

"Had you forgotten how he'd insisted on giving me the key?"

"That was what bothered me, what made me feel certain he had known uncle was up there. I still thought someone had been trying to frame him. I don't see how I could have been such a fool."

"We all make mistakes. God knows I've—"

"This other man," she said. "What did you mean when you said to Jeff just now 'If he's managed to discover why Frunk is after Tailholt'? That sounds as though you believe there might—"

"Wait," I said, and took a look out the door. The others were standing round the collar, talking among themselves while they waited for us to join them. "You may as well get this straight in your mind. There's only two reasons why Frunk would be after Tailholt. Either it's richer than Bender makes out to think or it's got Signal Stope apexed."

"Apexed!" She was staring at me thunderstruck, unable or unwilling—as I myself had been at first—to fully realize the implications.

"But . . . but an 'apex'," she exclaimed breathlessly, "is the end edge, or crest of a vein where that vein lies nearest the surface—"

"Under mining laws, as Bender can tell you, the owner of an apex may follow the vein or lode on its dip to any depth or distance within the prolonged end lines of his claim, *even though it enter adjoining lands.*"

"But Dad would have known!"

"He wasn't given much time. Signal Stope, from what I can find, has been going all out from the very first. Your father wasn't given much time to find anything. What he found originally may have only been float. He was killed before he'd done much development. Would you say Bender's estimate of Tailholt was accurate?"

"You mean the worth of our ore? Yes, I think so. It doesn't compare with the chunk on display at Frunk's Mercantile. If the rest of his mine is as good as that sample—"

"It probably isn't. But comparatively, at least, it may be extremely valuable. Say it is, and Frunk discovers your mine has him apexed. His natural reaction is to try to buy Tailholt before you discover the truth of the business. Another reaction would be to get all he can *while he can* out of Signal Stope. A third step which might naturally follow would be an all-out effort to retard Tailholt's development. You begin to get the picture now, don't you?"

She said, aghast: "Jeff Bender's a mining engineer! He must have known. . . ."

"He must certainly have suspected."

"You think he's the 'other man'?"

"I don't know," I told her honestly. "I don't know how far down he's put Tailholt or how much the workings show at this point. But I mean to find out. That's one of the reasons—"

"But you told him you weren't an authority—"

"A man doesn't have to be an authority on ore to know whether or not a mine's being swindled. You tell me Bender's an expert. I'm no expert, but with all this hanky-panky goin' on I've got sense enough to know the mine's worth more than he says it it. If he's right about the ore then you've got Frunk apexed. I'm pretty sure you have, and I'm sure Bender knows it. I think that's why he got rid of your crew; he can't afford to have anyone around he can't trust. The ore thieves are still doing business, so those guards and that fence have only one purpose—they're insurance that you don't find out what's going on."

She looked like hell. I could see that she believed me. "You think he knew about Joe?"

"He must have known Joe was working for Frunk or he wouldn't have let him inside of that fence. He *did* let him in. He even left Joe by himself here—"

"Perhaps he believed Joe was a Ranger. After all, Joe fooled *me*."

"Bender's no fool," I said. "He's in this thing right up to his neck. Either he's the 'other guy' or he has sold out to Frunk and to the other guy also. Frunk couldn't operate without Jeff's connivance. If this mine has Frunk apexed—"

"But how will you find out?"

"I'll know when I get down there."

"Don't you think Jeff suspects—"

"Of course. He knows I'm forcing his hand."

She looked at me oddly. "And you would still go down?"

"It's the best chance I've got of clearing this mess up—"

"But it's suicide! Don't you see that Jeff will tip Crafkin off?"

"He'll try, all right—"

"He's probably done it already!"

"In front of Bucks Younger? I don't think so. Younger's *my* insurance."

TWENTY

Younger, nodding to Carolina, politely took off his hat. "You've had a rough deal here, ma'am. I hope we can get to the bottom of this business."

He reached out his hand. "How are you, Trammell? Glad to have you with us. They tell me you're a Ranger, that we're going to search the mine."

"I don't know how much searching we'll do but I'm going to have a whack at it."

"I doubt," Crafkin said, "if it will do much good. I went down yesterday. The stopes are a mess. Blocked tunnels everywhere and—I suppose it's your notion the ore is still down there?"

"I'm convinced it never went out by the gate."

Bender grunted. "Where do you imagine it went out?"

"As Joe just said, it may still be down there. Behind those blocked tunnels maybe."

"If it is," Crafkin growled, "it'll be there till hell freezes. Wait'll you see them."

Younger looked thoughtful. "We're to hunt for the stolen ore then—is that it?"

"We're going to look," I said, "for evidence that this mine has Frunk's mine apexed."

There was a moment of intense quiet. Crafkin's head came round very carefully. The marshal's lips scrinched a silent whistle. A derisive amusement gleamed in Bender's stare. "All right, Hawkshaw," he nodded. "I'll help you look for that with real pleasure."

Younger twisted his yellow mustache. "You don't think there's anything to it?"

"On the contrary I find it remarkably intriguing. As a theory," Bender emphasized, "it's the solution magnificent. It would explain so credibly all that's been going on; but—"

"If that was the answer," Crafkin said, "you would have found it."

"Exactly. And I don't mind admitting I considered it myself. The facts, unfortunately, fail to cooperate. I've examined the face of the cuts repeatedly. I have found no evidence in support of the theory." He regarded me blandly. "You will have to assume I've miscalculated the valve of our ore, I guess, Trammell."

I looked at him straightly. "I have considerable respect for your professional skill, Bender; a great deal too much to imagine you have made any mistake of that kind."

"What type of operation do you have in the stopes?" Younger asked. "Cut and fill? Horizontal or incline?"

Bender said, "Cut and fill's much too costly for a mine of this kind. This is open stope mining. We're using the panel method."

"How far are you down?"

"Two hundred foot level—"

"You mean in all this time you've only driven three headings?"

Bender's cheeks went deeply roan. But he got hold of his temper. "I think that's pretty good progress, everything considered. Three men can't very well—"

"But Krole was working a big crew—"

"Krole quit work six months ago. When Shellman took over we were working twenty-five men. Within three weeks the crew dwindled to twelve. When I cut it to three for lack of money to pay them we quit going down. We've been working Number 2—"

"We'll go down," I said. "Get the lamps, will you, Bender?"

The mine boss, muttering under his breath, started off. "Get one for me, too," Carolina called after him.

Bender turned, still scowling, and said, "A mine is no

place for a woman, Miss Krole." And Younger said, "That's right. You'd better wait up here."

"Your crew wouldn't like it," Crafkin told her. "Miners think it's bad luck to have a woman—"

"A little more bad luck won't even be noticed," Carolina said grimly. "Fetch a lamp for me, Bender."

The mine boss shrugged and went on. I said to Carolina, "Hadn't you better change your clothes?"

"They look as good as yours," she said, and grinned at me tiredly. No one else said anything until the marshal, who'd been regarding my torn clothes curiously, asked, "What happened to you, Trammell?"

I told him about Irick's bunch chasing me through the brush.

He frowned. "You'd better pin your badge on—"

I cut in, asking Crafkin: "Did you fetch my saddle?"

"It was the badge you wanted, wasn't it? The badge wasn't there." He actually looked regretful. "You want to borrow mine?"

"Maybe, you'd better." Younger said, "before somebody shoots you."

Crafkin passed it over. It was mine, all right. I pinned it on without remark.

Bender came out of the change house with an armful of miner's hats with carbide lamps attached. We lit the lamps and put the hats on, Carolina stuffing her hair inside hers. Bender led the way to the collar and we all climbed into the cage. I picked up the three shotguns, handed one of them to Younger, kept one for myself and tossed the other outside.

Crafkin's eyes narrowed. Bender grinned. He pulled the gate down, gave a yank on the cable and the cage began its creaking descent. Increasing darkness accompanied our clattering slow-motion progress. At the 65-foot level, where the original heading had been widened out to form the first stope, the ring of radiance thrown from our carbide lamps showed nothing but the shapes of ghostly pillars. No sign of a back wall was visible.

"Having any trouble with water?" I asked Bender.

"We're not down far enough to be bothered by water We've got a little at 200."

We dropped below the second level. Conversation lagged as the walls of the shaft closed round us again. Dampness was beginning to spot them in patches that were like running sores where they gleamed in the passing light of our lamps. "I was under the impression," Bucks Younger remarked, "that you were working Number 2."

"That's right." Bender stopped the cage and sent the gate clattering up. "We have been. But any search we're going to make had ought to start at the bottom. This is it," he said. "The 200-foot level."

The quiet was uncanny. The monstrous shadows engulfed the wan glimmer of our lights with the stealth of gloved hands. I decided as we climbed out after him it was the weirdest damn place I had ever been in. The blackest, too. And the most oppressive.

The air was heavy with the stench of stale blasts. "What's the width of this cut?" asked the marshal, peering.

"Roughly thirty-five feet. Those pillars were left at thirty foot intervals."

"When'd you stop work here?" I asked curiously.

"About ten weeks ago."

"Why?" That was Younger.

"Number of reasons. We lost the vein, for one thing. It was while we were cross-cutting, trying to pick it up again, that the cave-ins I told you about started."

Did you pick it up again?"

The circle of his light bobbed as Bender nodded. The walls it illumined showed stained with damp in gangrenous splotches whose leakage was collected in the stagnant pools which leveled the floor's hollows with the green shine of slime.

"Where?" Younger asked.

"In Tunnel 14."

"Why aren't you working there now then?" Carolina asked. And Younger's eyes probed the mine boss's face. "Why'd you quit?"

"It was the crew that quit, not me," Bender grunted. "That's the tunnel we lost all the timbers out of. There's some running ground in it and we had to retimber. I shored it up twice and each time they were stole again—"

"Between dark and dawn?" I cried, incredulous.

"That's right," Bender nodded. "After the last time they pulled the sticks out of it I couldn't get posts big enough for the uprights. Not a man of the crew would go in the damn tunnel—"

"I'll go in it," I growled.

Bender's turning head flung his light in my face. "You won't for some while," he said grimly. "The whole ceiling dropped out of it two weeks ago—that's why we moved up into Number 2. That tunnel's nothing but a memory."

In the sepulchral hush I got one of the answers I'd been hunting for. The means by which a smart guy like Bender had figured to get away with the job he was doing. I'd been right as rain. Tailholt *did* have Frunk apexed but, if Bender was slick enough for this kind of dodge, it was a cinch he'd been cute enough to fix up the rest of it. We would find no proof of any apex down here.

The vein, to afford proof, would have had to dip toward Signal Stope, and I believed that it did. But if the vein had been recovered at the south end of 14, as Bender would have us believe, it was inconceivable that Frunk, in his Signal Stope, was gouging ore from the extended end lines of Tailholt's claim. Frunk's mine abutted Tailholt on the north and I was pretty well convinced this stope's north wall would tell us nothing; but I meant to make sure.

I turned my light in that direction. As it crossed Bender's face I saw the corners of his mouth quirk. He knew what I was up to. He was really enjoying this. "Nothing over there," he said. "When I was thinking, like you, that we might have Frunk apexed I had the whole crew working there; we moved tons of waste before I gave up the notion. You can see for yourself. We cleared—"

"Where's your up-set from this level?"

"Down this way," Bender said, heading into the western

gloom of the stope. We followed him approximately two hundred feet. Taking the lamp off his hat he directed its light upward. We could see the gaping hole where a raise had been driven to the level above for ventilation.

"All right," I said, "let's see your blocked tunnel."

Again we followed him through the crouching shadows between the roof-supporting pillars which divided the silent stope into an appearance of empty rooms. The sound of our boots clattered eerily and when Crafkin cleared his throat the echoes flew down the passages with the rumble of a landslide.

"Here it is," Bender said—"all that's left of it."

It was in the south face of the stope all right. The light of our lamps gave ample evidence there had actually been a tunnel, but it was so crammed with fallen rock and shale it would be a lengthy and costly operation to reopen it. Not, of course, that there would be any reason to.

"How far in did you go?" I asked Bender, knowing mighty well the whole damn tunnel wasn't nothing but a hoax.

"One hundred and thirty-eight feet."

"You're quite a gambler,'" I said dryly. "Why didn't you tunnel north?"

"Because, like you, I figured the stope dipped north. Every time we touched off a round I was sure the clean-up would show us in ore again."

"So then you used a crystal ball, drove a tunnel south and hit it, eh?"

"Not exactly," Bender grinned. "Number 14 was the fourth we drove on this level—"

"What happened to the other three?"

"Maybe you better take a look for yourself."

"Maybe I had at that," I said, and set off between the pillars toward the north wall again.

He called, "Not over there," but I ignored him.

The way I had this figured Tailholt *did* have Frunk's mine apexed. It was the only answer that made any sense, the reason I'd insisted on this search in the first place. I wasn't expecting to find any proof. I was going through the motions in the hope that it might drive them into making some fool move that would give me the proof I needed.

I was convinced Frunk's mine was apexed. If Bender's estimate of Tailholt's worth was right, Signal Stope must obviously be worth a considerable plenty or Frunk wouldn't have started all this hanky-panky. And he couldn't have got this far without help.

Now who, I asked myself, was the most logical guy to provide that help? All the signs and signal smokes pointed arrow-straight at Bender. As mine boss of Tailholt he had a better than even chance to get away with it. But he wouldn't play catspaw for peanuts. Even if he hadn't uncovered any proof he was bound to suspect this mine had Frunk apexed; he may even have pointed that out to Frunk. These two had obviously come to some agreement. Bender was quite able to add four and six.

But why would he have told Carolina he didn't believe Tailholt had much of a future? The answer to that was what finally had convinced me there was more than one skunk in this woodpile. By telling the girl the truth about the worth of her ore he probably hoped, when the time came, to buy the property cheap. He could then bid himself in as Frunk's full partner.

I'd gotten this far in my figuring before I'd sent Crafkin off to hunt Younger. By the time they'd returned I'd been reasonably confident Frunk would have learned the guards were off duty. It should have moved him to action. I didn't consider Frunk any bigger fool than Bender. He'd be forced to move to protect himself and, unless he were an idiot, he'd be bound to realize the menace of Bender.

This was the thing I was building my hopes on, to get him and Bender to try to outfox each other.

Still thinking about this I cut back in the direction of the up-cast, hearing the rest of them sloshing behind me. I flashed my lamp along the roof until I found it, then turned right and reached the stope's north face. I took my time and went over it thoroughly, thinking all the while about

Bender's duplicity and trying my damndest to guess what
he'd do next.

He was going to have to do something and do it pretty
soon. Before he could do anything he would have to slip away
from us, and he couldn't slip away from us without some
kind of diversion. He would have to manage something that
would draw our eyes away from him . . . or would he?
Was there any chance he'd dare to wait for Gid Frunk's
move?

He might if he were cool enough. It could give him a
considerable advantage, especially if he could get Frunk
caught and keep his own hand covered. If he could get
Frunk caught by Frunk's own actions, and devise some
means for keeping Frunk from talking, it would leave Jeff
Bender sitting very neat indeed.

Still busily examining the stope's north face I switched
my thinking to the stolen ore. How could they have gotten
it out of this mine? Even if all Bender's guards had been
in on it the stuff was too bulky to be handled with ease.
Crafkin had suggested the ore might still be down here and
perhaps he'd told the truth. It might have been loaded into
one of these blocked tunnels—into 14, maybe, before they'd
blasted it shut.

"Shut . . ." I muttered, and looked at the wall more
careful.

If Tailholt had Frunk apexed the slope of the vein's dip
would have had to go north, as I'd been thinking. Now supposing Bender had never lost the vein at all but had followed it north into Frunk's Signal Stope? Or had come head-
on smack into a Frunk tunnel? Tailholt ore, going into such
a tunnel, could come out of Frunk's mine at Signal Stope
ore and no one be the wiser.

Was that too far fetched?

To me it didn't seem so. All they actually needed was
some kind of concealed door, something that when shut
would appear to be solid wall.

I was sure I had the answer.

After sloshing back to the ventilator I went over the stope's north wall again, paying no attention to the remarks of the others, flashing my lamp from various angles across its blast and pick scarred surface. I found no indication of what I was hunting for. I saw a lot of cracked rock but none that looked to have been fitted in place again to mask a hidden opening.

I still liked my notion.

The others followed me back to the shaft.

"We'll try the next level now," I said, and was making ready to step into the cage when a shout stopped the bunch of us dead in our tracks.

TWENTY-ONE

CRAFKIN'S breath made an insucked sound as he swung beefy shoulders half around to peer at Bender. The mine boss' cheeks showed the shine of sweat. The shadows seemed to creep in closer and the marshal, looking hard at Bender, said in a voice turned thin with suspicion, "What the hell are you up to?"

Bender's eyes stared back unblinking, but there was an accent of nervousness about him now and something aroused was tightening the skin folded over his cheekbones.

His lips rolled and squeezed and then opened but, before he could speak, a frantic scream came churning up out of the stope's crouching shadows. It had the dying-woman sound that is sometimes torn from an injured horse.

I felt my flesh turn cold and crawl as, with the rest, I whirled to stand tumultuously peering into that wavering blackness beyond the reach of our lamps.

Here was the diversion Bender must have been praying

for, something to take our minds off him and allow him
those precious seconds he must have, if my guess concerning
his intentions held water. Yet there was no elation in the
way he stood staring. Visible strain rode his hunched-for-
ward shoulders and there was an underdone look to the fat
of his face that was strangely in contrast to its natural
appearance.

There may have been no especial significance in the way
Younger's shotgun was pointed at his middle but the
marshal's distrust was too open to be doubted. He was watching Bender as he would a snake.

"Lead off," he said dustily.

Bender did not move so much as a finger. "You fool!"
he cried. "That's Frunk up there—"

"Frunk, eh!" Younger's saturnine look branded Bender a
liar. Then, surprisingly, he laughed. "It won't wash, Jeff. I
wasn't born yesterday. You'll have to—"

"We've got to get out of here!" Bender yelled. "There's
something happening in Number 2—"

"Is it these stinkin' lights that make you look so yellow?"
Younger jeered, striding forward.

Bender fell back, his big hands fisted. His veins had
swelled with a curious rage and a wildness boiled up out of
his stare, yet he flung himself round without opening his
mouth, striding into the darkness like a cat through wet
grass, the beam of his lamp slashing this way and that
without turning up any sign of the screamer.

"Farther back," directed Younger as we went scrambling
after him. "It wasn't this close was it, Trammell?"

I'd been trying to guess how much of my figuring concerning Jeff Bender the marshal had caught up with and if
his suspicions coincided with mine. I wished I could have
managed to have talked with him privately before we'd
come down here, at least long enough to have told him what
bait I was setting out for these coyotes. I was putting his
head in a lion's mouth without even warning him the lion
might bite.

"I don't think so," I said. "Seemed to be nearer the far end of this wall, though it *could* have come out of that air hole—"

"It *could*," Younger grinned, "have come straight out of hell. But don't let our fat friend mislead you. That cry—"

"That cry," Bender snarled, sloshing back to us, "came out of Number 2 like I told you—you think I don't know how this mine distorts sound? If we don't get up there pretty goddam quick—"

The marshal's grin seemed about to give Bender apoplexy. He goggled, cheeks bloated, like a fish out of water.

Bucks Younger chuckled. "Careful, Jeff—"

"You crazy fool!" Bender shouted. "You want to be trapped in this goddam stope?"

"You should have stuck with the stage," Younger told him. "If I didn't know you so well you would have me scared stiff. But it's no good, Jeff; you might's well come off it. It was you that suggested we start on this level—"

"We goin' to wrangle all night?" cut in Crafkin. "That scream—"

"Wasn't nothing but stage dressing," the marshal said. "Window trimming. We've seen everything Jeff wanted us to, the rubble-blocked tunnel, the blast-scratched wall. He only fetched us here to convince us this mine couldn't have Frunk apexed. That scream was intended to rush us upstairs—"

"Stay down here then if you want Frunk to bury you!" Slamming Crafkin out of his way Bender bolted.

Younger, with a startled curse, leapt after him.

I was right at his heels, the others behind me. Even above the clatter of boots I could hear the rumble and whir of machinery. I redoubled my efforts. With the taste of defeat in my mouth I passed Younger, but the cage was already out of its berth and commencing the start of its creaking climb upward.

With a terrible cry Bender flung himself at it, got a foot on its floor edge, an arm through the wooden slats of its gate. Carolina screamed as the top of the cage vanished into the shaft. I tried to shut my eyes against the time when the stones of the stope's rocky ceiling must grind through the flesh and bones of his body.

But the stones never touched him. With the ceiling scant inches above the bulge of his body his fist caught the cable and with a clank the cage stopped. He jammed it into reverse and held it there, ashen, even after its bottom was grounded.

I let my breath go and rushed forward with Younger.

"Latch ahold of that cable," Bender wheezed, and I grabbed it above the gate until he got his arm out. Then he caught it underneath and Younger shoved the gate up and we all got aboard.

Sweat filmed Crafkin's dough white cheeks and Carolina's eyes looked as big as buckets. We were all pretty shaky I guess but the marshal. He said, tight and angry, "How did you know that was Frunk up there?"

"Know!" Bender snarled. "Who else would it be? Ain't you woke up yet that's what Trammell's been angling for?"

Younger's shoulders shifted. He brought his flushed face around savagely. But before he could put what he felt into words, something above us gave a twang and a slither and struck the cage roof with a hell of a clatter.

No one had to be told what the something was. There was enough of its sinuous length still twisting and kinking about the sides of the cage to tell its own story.

Frunk, or one of Frunk's hirelings, had taken the edge of an axe to the cable. My trap had been sprung and we were all caught in it. Two hundred feet below the earth's smiling surface.

TWENTY-TWO

YOUNGER'S blue eyes were not twinkling now. Temper showed in his cheeks and a hard held truculence looked out of the stare he flung at my face.

"I'm listenin'," he said as we got out of the cage.

I took him off to one side and explained this deal as I saw it. "So there's two guys after this mine, both of them bucking the owner and each of 'em trying to outsmart the other. Frunk, after making a rich strike in Signal Stope, discovers Krole's mine has him apexed. It's the only logical answer. Maybe Bender told him—it don't make much difference how the hell he found out. Except if Bender told him he would know right away he would have to deal with Bender. He would pretty near have to anyway. Bender, as Tailholt's manager, was in the key spot to make or break him. So they hatch up a deal."

Younger nodded. "I'll go with you that far."

"Then Bender," I said, "decides to grab the whole works. Secretly he helps Frunk put the skids under Tailholt. More secretly he manages to keep Frunk from wrecking it. We know this is true because the quickest and simplest way out for Frunk would be to blow this damn mine to hell and gone.

"Nothing but Bender has stood in his way. Bender didn't want that. The only real hold he could have on Frunk is proof that this mine has Frunk's mine apexed. That proof still exists or we wouldn't be down here. Obviously, then, Jeff Bender's Frunk's partner *and the man who has kept Frunk from putting this mine where it no longer threatens him*. Isn't that the way this thing looks to you?"

149

Younger said with a quick unaccustomed bluntness: "You're goddam right!" and his eyes shone like agate.

"So I pulled the guards off, knowing the word would get around. Long as Bender and Frunk sat tight I had no proof. I had to spur them to action. I thought the chance of trapping us down here might do it—and I had one other thought."

Younger nodded. "You thought to sell Frunk the notion Bender'd thrown in with us—"

"That was part of it," I said. "But I also figured Bender'd see that, too, and the good chance it gave him of turning the tables on Frunk. Bender saw it all right, only Frunk got going before he was ready—"

"And now your damn trap has backfired—"

"That's what my other thought was about. I thought if it did Bender'd get us out of it. If he hadn't known a way to get out of it himself he wouldn't have come down here with us in the first place."

Younger looked at me intently. "By God, I believe you're right. Come on. We'll twist the truth out of him. If you've outguessed the bastard we don't want to lose him."

That was my notion too but something subtly different about Bucks Younger's appearance dug into my thinking and sharpened my look as I returned his regard. I said, "Your light's going out."

He took off his hat, removed the lamp and shook it. Flaring briefly, the flame turned blue and went out. I watched the steel-spring fingers of Shafts' law take the lamp apart. There was nothing but sludge in its firebox.

Younger suddenly swore, but not at the lamp .He was peering toward where we had left the others. I turned too and something ugly started shinning up my spine.

There were no lights showing.

We broke into a run.

"What the hell?" Crafkin growled, and then my lamp picked them out of the roundabout blackness and I should have felt better.

Carolina's wan smile was a precious thing, but it didn't

help Younger. I saw his solid chin jump forward. "Where's Bender?" he snapped.

Eyes bulging, Crafkin fell back a step, his lips going white at their corners. "He was right here with us just a minute ago. Our lamps went out and—"

"You fool!" Younger snarled, and flung a black look at me. "You've fixed things now with your goddam meddling! If your guess was right that sidewindin' polecat—"

I grabbed Joe Crafkin by the front of his shirt but it was Carolina's voice that cut into the marshal's. "He can't have gone far. Our lamps went out just about the time yours did. We were—"

"Listen!" I said, and we all held our breaths but we didn't hear any clatter of bootsteps. Younger's cheeks turned livid with the rage that was in him. The skin of the hand that was gripping his shotgun showed ridged with tension.

And then I remembered. "The up-cast!" I cried, and Crafkin tore from my grip and dashed off snarling curses.

We were right on his heels when he got there. This gaping black hole was the means by which blast fumes were carried out of this level, and I knew it was the practice in mines to sometimes use such vents for pipelines, though there weren't any pipes coming down out of this one. The stope's ceiling here was hardly more than five feet above the floor and right under the hole was a two-foot block of gray sandstone which had obviously been left there for emergencies.

I caught Crafkin's shoulder before he could mount it. "Wait!" I growled, and again we listened.

There was somebody in that dark up-cast all right; we could hear the distant sounds of his climbing.

Across the bones of his face Crafkin's skin was stretched like parfleche. With a snarl he twisted out of my grasp and would have jumped to the block if the marshal's fist had not knocked him sprawling. Younger said through his teeth: "If anyone's going to get out of this mess it will be Miss Krole and not a dog like you."

Crafkin's look was rank as he picked himself up. I thought for a moment he meant to grab for his gun. In the light of my lamp he looked tough and ugly. He said in a cotton-soft voice, "I'm not forgettin' that. No man lays a hand on a Ranger—"

"That's enough," I said. "Unbuckle your gun belt and let it drop, Joe."

He turned his head slowly. "This is no time for horse-play—"

"Drop that belt or *I*'ll drop you."

He took in the leveled glint of my shotgun, considered me briefly and saturninely shrugged. "There's a new fool born every minute, I reckon." He let his gun-weighted belt fall into the muck.

I kicked it aside. "Get moving," I said. "You ain't foolin' nobody."

He stared at us blankly. "I don't get it."

"You will if Bender starts throwing lead—"

"Good lord," he cried, "you don't think I'm in cahoots with him, do you?" He looked genuinely astonished. "Have you fellows gone loco?" He slanched a hard glance at me. "What do you suppose Cap Murphey will say when—"

"Never mind Murphey. Get up on that block and—"

"By God," Crafkin said, "have you thrown in with these crooks?" Disbelief and a half-convinced loathing looked out of the stare he fixed on my face. The whole job was so good I'd half started to wonder if I'd doped this all wrong when Younger's short laugh fetched me up with a jerk.

"Another damn actor," he said with a contempt that conjured up a vision of Gharst wilting into the dust of the street while this slick-talking scorpion scuttled up that black alley. "Get into that hole," Younger growled, "and start climbing!"

Crafkin's glance sought Carolina's. "You can see through this, can't you? You understand what they're up to? Younger, as you've thought all along, is in with Frunk, and now he's talked Trammell into backing their—"

"You're just wastin' your breath," I said. "She knows better than to believe any hogwash like that. You killed Gharst and all the slick yarns you can spin won't change that, and it makes no difference that it was me you were after. Murder is murder and your hands are red with it. You killed Shellman Krole—"

"You must think folks are fools if you think they'll swallow that! You will find," he said with a great show of scorn, "it takes more than words to hang a frame on—"

I rammed the shotgun's muzzle hard against his belly. "Get up into that hole and start crawling, you skunk!"

"Get that thing out of my guts," he said savagely. "You ain't shootin' nobody. I ain't taking that rap for you, either. Carolina—"

"No," she said, drawing away from him. "I trusted you once. Even then I was desperately afraid you had done it. No one else had half the oppor—"

"I can explain about that—"

"You've told enough lies now," Younger growled, seizing hold of him. "You're not keeping us talking till that lamp burns out. Get into that hole before I knock your damn face off!"

Crafkin's eyes turned ugly but he climbed into the hole.

Thinking Younger may have guessed the truth of the matter I had the lamp off my hat and was about to blow it out when he stopped me. "Leave it lit," he said grimly. "Bad as we may get to need that light I don't fancy crawlin' up that air vent in the dark. I want to be able to see what the vinegarroon's up to. You want Miss Krole to go next?"

"You better go next," I said, "and keep an eye on him. If I keep right behind you I think you'll be able to see enough to drop him if you have to."

I was telling him that mostly for its effect on Crafkin who might very well have been figuring out some more skulduggery to try on us in the darkness of the air vent.

I climbed into the up-cast after the marshal and, wedging myself to get purchase, I hauled Carolina into it after me. It was the blackest hole I had ever been in, with the shadows like ink where my lamp failed to cut them. The way led sharply upward, angling this way and that around great blocky boulders which the diggers of this shaft hadn't

bothered to remove. Because of these twisting convolutions
more than half the time we couldn't see Crafkin's shape at
all and sometimes I could not even see Younger. Bender,
I realized, must already have vanished into the black obscurity of the stope above and the thought of what he might
be doing was not calculated to make me forget the tons
of rock hanging over us. Only a very short length of ignited
fuse might very well lie between ourselves and eternity.

Younger wasn't making any study of geology. He was
moving just as fast as he was able to, and we were right on
his heels but, even where we were able to do more than
crawl, our pace was hardly faster than a turtle's. In several
places the walls were pressed so close by unremoved boulders
we had to wriggle to get past, but if Bender could make
it I knew we could.

Then Younger's face came around and eyed me over his
shoulder. "Only five feet left." With great care and no
sound his lips shaped the words. "Crafkin's not in sight. Better put that lamp out.

There was good sense in the suggestion but it wasn't
needed. Even as I took the lamp off my hat its light flared
and faded and with a splutter went out. Pitch darkness
hemmed us in with our terrifying thoughts.

In that blackness I heard the distant sound of someone
walking. Carolina put a hand on my leg; I felt her shudder.
Then the sound was lost in the nearer sound of the marshal's
resumed progress. Through the absolute blackness I began
crawling after him, expecting any moment to hear the shat-
tering explosion that would bury us in this damned place
forever.

My mouth was drier than a barnful of cotton.

In sudden desperation I increased my pace but my out-
stretched hand did not find Bucks Younger. It did not touch
any wall nor did my other hand, either. I regrasped my
shotgun and got to my feet as quiet as I was able with one
hand over my head vainly feeling for a ceiling which was
not within reach. I knew in that moment I was out of the
up-cast with my feet on the floor for the Number 2 stope.

I wanted mightily to reestablish contact with Younger but, with Crafkin and possibly Bender somewhere in the dark about me, I dared not speak lest betrayal of my position loose a blast of hot lead.

With extreme care I felt ahead of me with one exploring foot. It came up against something and I felt the something sway away. I bent carefully downward and my extended left hand found an empty boot and, beside it, a second boot. Also empty.

Whose boots? Bender's? Or were they Crafkin's or Younger's?

I listened for Carolina but there was no sound behind me. I crouched down on one knee and felt around some more and, one by one, I got hold of four more boots.

I didn't like it. I didn't like any of the thoughts those boots conjured. The menace in this blackness was rank enough to taste. I was certain I wasn't alone. I was even more certain that I should get hold of Carolina and make some immediate attempt to get out of this black hole. I was fairly trembling with it yet I was rooted where I crouched by the equally certain conviction that the first sound I made would draw gunfire.

With infinite caution I put down my shotgun and quietly eased the .45 from my holster. With left hand, then, I picked up a boot and flung it ahead with all the strength I could muster. It struck with a splash and not a damn thing happened.

I don't know how long I stayed motionless. Time stood still in that impenetrable blackness. The silence had begun to churn up my nerves when I gradually became aware that something near me was breathing with a careful stealth that matched my own.

I dared not fire lest it be the marshal.

I dared not speak lest it be someone else.

With jaws clamped together I determined to outwait him, but the recurring vision of all those tons of rock got the best of me. I could not understand why Frunk hadn't caved this mine in already. He might be lighting a fuse someplace even now.

The thought brought cold sweat and, reaching down my left hand, I gathered up three more boots and heaved them altogether in the same direction I had thrown the first.

For a couple of heartbeats it was just like before with the sounds dying into a cold breathless silence. Then a lance of flame whitely knifed the murk, three other gouts bursting almost simultaneously. Crafkin's scream was swallowed in the bang-banging echoes.

After that there was no sound beyond the awful whimper of his strangling sobs which grew fainter and fainter and finally ceased entirely.

Still unfired I gripped my own gun and waited. Crafkin's gun was in the stope below, yet three guns had spoken—one of them twice. Had Crafkin had a second gun cached away on him someplace or had there been four men in this stope besides myself? It was a question that gnawed at me and another kept it company. If there had been a fourth was the fourth man Frunk?

One of those guns had gone off very near me and had probably been fired by the man I'd heard breathing, but the most I had seen was the gray wraith of a shape forward crouched above the flash. No details—nothing at all by which I could fasten a name to him.

I thought it might be the marshal but I couldn't be sure.

Wherever she was, I hoped Carolina would have enough savvy to keep down and keep her mouth shut.

I thought to catch the faint pad·of bare feet moving someplace, but again I couldn't be sure and would not have dared fire if I had been. I was all too aware that Carolina was probably behind me, that any slug meant for me might as easily tag her. A faint click seemed to come out of the distance and a draft crossed my face very briefly as though a door had been opened and when, shortly later, a soft thud came out of that yonder blackness I knew that one had, and that the door now was closed.

I heard the faint crunch of shale to my right and looked

that way and, of course, saw nothing. Every muscle in my body was stretched so taut I could hardly breathe. Both my legs were cramped and one foot was asleep. I had to move soon or I would be unable to. The thought of escape just then seemed very sweet to me—all the sweeter since I knew I'd never leave without the girl. If I could find that door. . . .

I sat down and with my pistol in my lap very quietly pulled my boots off. I wiggled my toes until feeling returned to the foot that had gone to sleep. Gun in hand again I rose and, keeping well behind the place where I'd heard that fellow breathing, I commenced a cautious travel in the direction from which I'd thought to feel that draft.

I wondered if all this fatigue and excitement were not tending perhaps to unbalance my mind. Mines is this country didn't have doors. If there was one in these dark reaches it could have but one purpose, to conceal a connection between this mine and Frunk's.

Now another queer fancy got to chousing my thoughts. I couldn't see a thing but I began to feel certain that somewhere in this stope someone else was moving toward the same spot I was. I had never felt anything as strongly before.

I tried to guess what the fellow was up to and, by that, determine which one of them it was. Perhaps he'd heard or sensed my movement and was making this trek in an attempt to cut me off. Or was he, unaware of my intention, heading this way on the same purpose I was? Maybe what I needed was a good string of spools. Or a nice quiet place to pick the lint off my clothing.

If there *had* been a fourth man in this stope, if that draft had been the sign of his departure and the man had been Gid Frunk himself, would he have taken such a risk for nothing? I had no way of gauging how long we'd been underground but it didn't seem possible he'd just now be returning from his trip to axe the cable. He might, however, have been completing his arrangements for setting off a blast. He would not have needed to light any fuse if he had a good battery and a sufficient length of wire. . . .

That thought brought the sweat cracking through my
skin again but common sense assured me that a man smart
as Frunk was would hardly have cut that cable if he'd meant
to blow the mine up. What he probably had been doing was
caving in the air vent between this level and the stope
above. Then, with his trick door shut and himself on the
farther side of it—

A fragment of sound, as from a bit of scuffed shale, laid
hold of my attention like the crack of a whip. Something
had moved just ahead and to the left of me and, even as
I dropped to a crouch on my hunkers, I again heard that
click lancing out of the darkness. A slight wind came with it,
whispering of death as it crossed my ankles, and blinding
light as a section of the wall swung at right angles, outward.
Caught flat-footed in the glare of three lamps Jeff Bender
stood with a gun in each fist.

Younger, three feet away, abruptly jerked both triggers of
his double-barreled shotgun and, when neither barrel spoke,
hurled the weapon at Bender. In that moment, when time
seemed crazily to stand completely still, I remembered the
smugness of the mine boss' grin when I had given that sawed-
off to Younger.

He ducked and fired from both fists and his face turned
choleric when the marshal wouldn't fall. You could see those
big slugs biting into the man, shaking and twisting him,
smashing him backward, but he wouldn't go down. With
his eyes like obsidian, with a terrible, implacable single-
ness of purpose, Younger's hand reached his belt and without sign of hurry lifted the sleek double-action from its
holster and had almost tipped it level when he went down
as though pole-axed in a blast from the tramcar.

Something jerked at my sleeve, something slapped at
my vest. As I flung myself prone on the stope's barren floor
I saw Bender spin and Irick's face just beyond him suddenly
jerk its mouth wide and fade howling from sight into the
blackness behind him. I hardly felt the gun bucking against
my palm in recoil. From back of me somewhere Carolina's
pistol made swift crashes of sound and Short Creek, leap-

ing from the car in wild panic, collapsed in mid air like a pricked balloon.

The reverberations were deafening. The stope was rank with the stench of burnt powder; stringers of blue smoke hung like clouds across the pitiless glare of the carbide lamps. Bender lay where he had fallen beside the open tunnel door, wheezing his life away besides the still shape of the town's dead marshal.

I retched, looking at them—I just couldn't help it.

Carolina called my name. I heard the crunch of her boots as she picked her way toward me. But I made no move or answer because something else was moving with an inch by inch stealth just back of the lamps that were affixed to the tramcar. I saw the barrel of a pistol edging out of the blackness and knew its baleful focus was being fixed on Carolina. I drove a slug just behind it and, with a snarling curse, Frunk reeled into view clutching his right shoulder with blood reddened fingers.

I jumped to my feet and as his gangling shape bent to retrieve the dropped pistol I put five knuckles hard against his bearded jaw.

"THAT's all there was to it," I told Cap Murphey two days later. "We tied him up and by the time he came to I had found Gharst's wife and got all the dope I needed. It was her scream we'd heard. She was in with him hand and glove until she found out I was in that mine with the rest of them. She knew what his plans were and tried to get me out. He caught her opening that secret door they'd rigged between the two mine tunnels. He hit her with an axe but she lived long enough to testify. Carolina heard her story and took it down and had her sign it.

"I had the most of it figured fairly close to the facts, but that guy Younger had me fooled from the start. It was him that was really playing hell with Frunk's plans but he was so damn slick I never caught on until I saw him throw down on Bender with that shotgun. Bender'd looked pretty

smug when I had handed Bucks that gun and when I realized
he must have pulled the loads from the thing, the whole
deal fell into focus. Bender, of course, knew exactly what the
score was.

"A dog-eat-dog business," I said with a scowl. "What
really threw the wrench in the works was me getting rid
of those guards of Bender's. I had him over a barrel on
that one—those birds were his personal life insurance; he
hired them to keep Frunk and Younger off his neck. He must
have hated like hell to see them heading for town but he
couldn't protest without exposing his hand."

"Well, you made your mistakes," Cap said, thinking it
over, "but you got the job done. I suppose you're figuring
to turn in your badge—"

"What give you that notion?"

"Well, that girl's going to need a man to—"

"Do I look that foolish?" I said, shoving my chin out.
"That gal was born to trouble. I don't want any part of her.
I'm goin' to get me a place in the Organ Mountains where
I can hunker in the shade and watch the horses switch flies.
No women for me—an' no more Rangerin'."